Earl Sewell

Keysha's Drama

KIMANI
tru
™

KEYSHA'S DRAMA

ISBN-13: 978-0-373-83079-4
ISBN-10:   0-373-83079-3

www.KimaniTRU.com

Printed in U.S.A.

FRESH. CURRENT. AND TRUE TO YOU.

Dear Reader,

What you're holding is very special. Something fresh, new and true to your unique experience as a young African-American! We are proud to introduce a new fiction imprint—Kimani TRU. You'll find Kimani TRU speaks to the triumphs, problems and concerns of today's black teens with candor, wit and realism. The stories are told from your perspective and in your own voice, and will spotlight young, emerging literary talent.

Kimani TRU will feature stories that are down-to-earth, yet empowering. Feel like an outsider? Afraid you'll never fit in, find your true love or have a boyfriend who accepts you for who you really are? Maybe you feel that your life is a disaster and your future is going nowhere? In Kimani TRU novels, discover the emotional issues that young blacks face every day. In one story, a young man struggles to get out of a neighborhood that holds little promise by attending a historically black college. In another, a young woman's life drastically changes when she goes to live with the father she has never known and his middle-class family in the suburbs.

With Kimani TRU, we are committed to providing a strong and unique voice that will appeal to *all* young readers! Our goal is to touch your heart, mind and soul, and give you a literary voice that reflects your creativity and your world.

Spread the word…Kimani TRU. True to you!

Linda Gill
General Manager
Kimani Press

For my uncle Larry Studway

There will never be anyone as unique as you.

Acknowledgments

First of all I must thank God for all of my blessings and for the gift of creativity. I want to thank the students at Bret Harte Middle School in Chicago, Illinois, Avondale Junior High School in Atlanta, Georgia, McKinnely Junior High in South Holland, Illinois, and Palatine High School in Palatine, Illinois, for giving me an opportunity to share my love of creative writing.

To Candice Sewell for being a constant inspiration in my life. I love you more than you'll ever know.

To Ms. Saleen Alan for being such a passionate and inspirational teacher to your students.

To Lisa Johnson for helping me to see this project through to the end. Thank you for all of your help.

To Mary Griffin for getting on my case when I slide offtrack or fall behind on my writing schedule.

To Annette McNair, Martina Royal and Donna Hill, thank you for your willingness to offer help at the drop of a dime.

To Linda Gill, Glenda Howard and Evette Porter for the opportunity to be a part of the Kimani TRU imprint.

To Sisters on the Reading Edge Book Club in Antioch, California, and Circle of Sisters Book Club in Kalamazoo, Michigan, for all of the love and support you've shown me.

To Fred Miller, John Rossini and Steve Rossini for your friendship over the years and for providing me with an opportunity to return to Palatine High School as a guest speaker at the boys and girls' track-and-field banquet. Speaking to the students was very rewarding.

To everyone who has supported my work over the years, thank you so much for helping me make my dream a reality.

To my readers—I'd love to know what you think about this book. Please forward your messages to earl@earlsewell.com. Please be sure to put the title of the book in the subject line so that I'll know your message to me is not spam e-mail.

"Anyone who has ever struggled with poverty knows how extremely expensive it is to be poor."

—James A. Baldwin

chapter 1

No matter how hard I tried to get Ronnie's attention he wouldn't look me. He avoided eye contact by toying with the ring tones on his cellular phone. His unwillingness to look me in the eye and speak directly to me annoyed me. Ronnie was seventeen and stood about five foot nine inches tall. He had brown skin just like mine and wore his hair French braided. That day he was wearing an oversize white T-shirt, baggy Sean John jeans and what appeared to be a new pair of Nike Air Force One gym shoes. We were standing on the sidewalk in front of the apartment building that he lived in with his mother. In the distance I heard the thud of music from a trunk amp bouncing against the air. Ronnie is my boyfriend, or should I say was my boyfriend until I caught him snuggled up with some girl inside of a movie theater. When I saw him and the other girl I decided to play it cool at first, you know, just to make sure that I wasn't overreacting. I discreetly positioned myself in a seat directly behind them so that I could keep a close eye on them. No sooner than the lights went down, Ronnie took off his jacket, hooked it around her shoulders and began kissing her. That's when I lost it. Before I could even think rationally, I began attacking them both. I slapped him on the head and pulled her hair. It wasn't long before two movie theater ushers rushed in to stop my assault as well as ask me to leave. At the time I didn't give Ronnie a chance to explain what was going on and who the girl was. To be honest, I really didn't care who she was. All I knew was that my boyfriend, who had told me at least twenty times he loved me the night before, wasn't acting like it.

The movie theater incident happened weeks ago. I hadn't seen or heard from Ronnie since that time because I had to move away due to a load of family drama that was going on in my life. During the time I was away, I cried a lot partly because of the situation my family was in and partly because I really missed Ronnie. Now that I'd returned to my old neighborhood, I thought for sure Ronnie had missed me at least a little. I also wanted to give him a chance to explain himself as well as see if we could forget about what happened in the past and start over. Besides, I'd heard that he was no longer with the girl he'd been caught cheating with.

I tried once again to get Ronnie to acknowledge me.

When our eyes finally met, I could tell he wanted me to disappear and forget that we ever had anything meaningful.

"Why did you even come around here looking for me?" he snapped at me as if the very sight of me irritated him like a bad skin rash.

"Don't you bark at me like that," I shouted back at him. "I thought you'd missed me and I wanted to give you a chance to explain yourself. So, what happened between us, Ronnie?" I asked straight out.

"I've already told you. It's over between us. You're playing too many games, girl. I'm just not into you anymore."

"But why? What did I do?"

"You're crazy for starters," Ronnie said and then was silent for a long moment as I waited for him to elaborate. "Look, you just need to forget you even know me. In fact, just erase my name and face out of your memory."

"How can you say that to me? After all we've been though? You told me you loved me and no matter what we'd be together. You promised me, Ronnie, you promised me that you'd never hurt my heart." I raised my voice at him. I couldn't help it because my heart was hurting. It didn't matter that we hadn't seen each other in two months, my heart was still broken and I wanted an explanation.

"Look, girl!" he said, pointing his index finger at me as if it was a weapon.

"Oh, now I'm just some girl?" Whenever I got upset about something, no matter how calm I tried to be my voice would always express how I truly felt. "Get your finger out of my face." I quickly grabbed his index finger and tried to twist it off his hand. I wanted to hurt him at that moment. I wanted him to feel the heartache and pain I felt. We tussled for a moment before he broke free of my grip.

"You need to leave, Keysha. I'm not playing with you. Go on back home to your mama."

"So what are you saying, Ronnie?"

"Keysha, I'm through with you. What part of that isn't getting through your thick skull?"

"How can you just turn your feelings for me off like that? I mean, I thought about how I felt about you every day. I even called you after the incident and left messages for you asking you to call me back so we could talk but you didn't. I even called you when I found out that I had to move away for a while. I thought for sure you'd at least want to know where I was being shipped off to but you never contacted me." I was pleading my case. I reminded him of my good-faith efforts to stick by his side. I was hoping that he'd feel some sense of guilt.

"Keysha, I'm just not feeling you like that anymore. You were cool for a minute but then you started smothering me. You called me too much, you didn't like it when I wanted to hang out with my friends instead of you. On top of that you're too bossy. I just can't get down with a girl that acts crazy and bossy all of the time. You need to roll out and leave me alone."

"Okay, I'll change. Will that help?" I asked, hoping to find the words he wanted to hear.

"No, just leave me alone, all right." Ronnie finally put away his cellular phone. "I've just erased your name, number and special ring tone from my phone. It's been real," he said and then turned his back and walked toward his building.

"I hate you, Ronnie!" I shouted out as loudly as I could. I wanted everyone within the sound of my voice to know how upset I was. I suddenly didn't care about making a public scene.

"Yeah, whatever. Don't come around here looking for me anymore," he said as he entered his building. At that moment rage pumped through my blood and I rushed into the building behind him. I grabbed a fistful of his pretty braided hair and tried to snatch it out of his head. He reached back and put his hand over my fist and tried to pry it away.

"Let go of my hair, Keysha!" he shouted out as we scuffled. At that moment I heard the door to his apartment open. Ronnie's mother came into the hallway above us on the next landing.

"Let him go before I call the police on you!" she screamed at me. Part of me didn't care if I went to jail but another part of me did. I held on to his hair for a moment longer and then yanked really hard, ripping his hair from his skull.

"Get out!" his mother commanded me. She was much larger than I was and for all my spunk I knew I was no match for her. "And don't let me catch you back around here anymore. Do you understand me?"

I rushed out of the building before Ronnie or his mother could come within arm's length of me. Once I got outside, I ran as fast as I could. I wanted to get away from them. In many ways, I wanted to run away from myself, but I knew that was impossible. When I finally stopped running, I was a good four blocks away. I decided to rest on a bus bench so I could catch my breath. I leaned forward and rested my elbows on my thighs as I waited for my breathing to regulate. For a moment, I thought about crying but I couldn't summon up any tears because I was too angry. My life was so messed up. I swear, sometimes I wondered if some mythical witch or wizard placed a curse on me. I swept my fingers through my hair as I mulled over my situation. My mother, Justine, was crazy as well as pregnant. I had to admit that it tripped me out when she admitted she was going to have a baby. Justine is a real piece of work. In fact, her brain should probably be donated to science because her thought process is completely twisted. My mom became pregnant with me when she was very young. She acts more like my girlfriend than my mom. She cares more about partying than she does about keeping a roof over our heads, a decent job or food on the table. Sometimes, well most times, we fought and argued with one another. I didn't like her because she didn't act her age and in some ways resented the day I was born. At least that's the way I felt.

A bus stopped in front of me, and the driver opened the door thinking that I wanted to get on. I looked at him for a moment and then waved him on. I sat upright on the bench and glanced at the green and white street sign. I was at the corner of Chicago and Laramie Avenues, which meant that I was in the heart of the hood. My mom and I were staying in a basement apartment a few blocks up. I hated the place. It was run down, dirty and infested with roaches and rats. It was nothing like my Aunt Estelle's home. She had a beautiful high-rise apartment overlooking Lake Michigan. I used to live there with her husband, Dr. Richard Vincent, my Grandmother Rubylee and my cousin Nathan. It was nice living in such a grand place, but that all changed because my Grandmother Rubylee, who was crazier than my mom, was stealing money out of Richard's bank account. She got caught by the police and is serving time for her crime. Shortly after my Grandmother Rubylee was arrested, my Aunt Estelle passed away, and that pretty much ended the welcome of Justine and me in Dr. Vincent's home. All of that happened about two months ago, right around the time I caught Ronnie at the movie theater with some girl.

* * *

I decided it was time to get up off the bus bench before I started to look like a female version of Forrest Gump. As I continued on my way home, I thought about school, which would be starting soon, but I wasn't looking forward to it, especially since my mother didn't have money for back-to-school gear. I knew kids were going to talk about me walking around in last year's fashions. I was real self-conscious when it came to fashion and my appearance. My face was filled with pimples and my hair was overprocessed from doing one too many home perms. I thought my nose was too big, my butt was too big, my breasts were too small and my legs were too skinny. I was thinking about my situation and self-image so hard that I actually walked past my apartment building and had to turn around and go back. The building was a large red brick structure with three separate entrances. I had to walk down the block a little ways to the very last entrance, which was near an alley and vacant lot where alley mechanics liked to park their hoopty-mobiles and work on them while they drank alcohol. If they couldn't get their cars running they'd just leave them there until they could. From time to time, if the cars sat too long, eventually parts would come up missing. The entrance to my building wasn't secure at all. The landlord got tired of putting locks on the doors because tenants or their guests continually kicked in the door to gain entrance. I think people did that sort of thing because they didn't have much else to do. I was about to enter the vestibule of the building when I heard someone call my name.

"Keysha, hold on a minute." I stepped back out into the sunlight and saw Toya Taylor, a friend that I'd known for years. She lived in the apartment across the hall from me. Toya had a baby she was continually trying to get neighbors to watch for her while she roamed the streets trying to keep up with her baby's daddy. Toya is sixteen but the father of her baby is a few years older than her. Toya was also rather conceited when it came to her hair. She was one of those girls who had a finer grade of hair as opposed to a coarser grade. She loved to show it off and brag about its length. Today for some reason, she wasn't in the mood to show off her hair because she had it tied up in a black head scarf.

"Hey, what's up? Why do you have on that head scarf? It's hot as hell out here." I was being nosy. I wanted to know what was going on with her hair.

"Girl, my baby's daddy is tripping. He doesn't like for me to be outside by myself with my hair down so he makes me tie it up when I'm not around him."

"Well, if it makes him happy then I guess it is okay," I said, even though I didn't believe her for one minute. I think she did something to her hair and now it's messed up and she doesn't want to get ridiculed for having damaged it.

"Where have you been? I came over looking for you this morning but you weren't home."

"Girl, I got into a fight with Ronnie," I said as I sat down on the step. Toya sat beside me.

"What about? You told him that you wanted to give him a chance to explain himself, right?"

"Yeah, I told him, but it didn't matter. He still treated me like I was a fly at a picnic. I got so mad at him that I pulled out a patch of his hair."

"For real?" Toya's voice was now filled with excitement. "What happened next?" she asked, wanting to know every detail.

"His mother came out into the hallway where we were," I said as I scratched my arm.

"You fought his mother, too?" Toya asked, jumping ahead of my story.

"No. I didn't fight his mother. When I saw her I turned and ran out of the building."

"So, are you sad about the breakup?" Toya asked. "Because if my baby's daddy broke up with me, it would be on. I'd have to hurt him." I wanted to point out the fact that I'd heard that her so-called man had another girl he was dealing with, but I didn't want to go there with her. I just wasn't in the mood to fight with anyone else right then.

"So, what's next? What are you going to do? You've got to find a new man."

"Girl, I'm not thinking about boys right now. I'm

thinking about school and trying to get through another year." I glanced up at a few billowy clouds and then down at my feet. My gym shoes had seen better days.

"I think I'm going to drop out of school," said Toya.

"Why do you want to drop out of school?" I asked, looking at her strangely.

"I can't find anyone to watch my baby. Do you know they want, like, eight hundred dollars a month to take care of my baby? I don't have that type of money. That's why I was really hoping that you were pregnant because we could've helped each other out. Maybe we could have gone to school part-time or something. While I was in class you could have babysat for me and vice versa. Our kids would've grown up together and been very close."

"You know, at first I wanted to be the mother of Ronnie's child because I thought it would bring Ronnie and me closer but now I don't. Especially after what happened today."

"Even if Ronnie wasn't around, you would've had me and we would've been close," Toya said but that didn't make me feel any better. Besides, I'm not sure if I would've ever left my baby with Toya. I mean, she did okay with her little boy, but I think caring for him was much more than she bargained for.

"So what are you going to do if you drop out?" I asked.

"I don't know. Probably sit around, play cards and collect a government check. I wouldn't have to worry about teachers or homework or anything. All I'd have to do is chill out." Toya began to bite her fingernails.

"Don't you think you'll get bored? Don't you want to make money and live in a big house, drive a nice car and have enough money to buy yourself some serious bling?" I asked.

"Girl, that's what a man is for. My boo is going to take care of me," she stated as if her life plan was rock solid. In her mind Toya had it all figured out. At times talking with Toya annoyed me because she didn't have any ambition. *At least I had that*, I thought to myself.

"I'm going to go inside. I'm starving," I said as I stood up.

"You want some company? Me and the baby could come over," Toya said.

"No, I'm cool," I answered her then walked inside of the apartment building. The last thing I wanted to do was hang out with Toya and her baby.

chapter 2

The apartment my mom and I lived in felt more like a big square box than a studio apartment. Once inside there really wasn't much to see. On the right wall was an old white stove that looked as if it'd come from the Stone Age. I was continually amazed that it actually worked. The refrigerator, which was next to the stove, was just as ancient. It was white with a chrome handle that had to be pulled toward your body before the door would open. There was one window at the back of the room. It looked out over the abandoned lot where the alley mechanics work and loiter. The window didn't have a curtain, just a dingy white shade. On the left side was the bathroom, which was long overdue for a makeover. Sometimes I was completely grossed out by the murky brown water that came out of the faucet. You had to let it run for a while before it changed color. Next to the bathroom was an oversize door, which was where the Murphy bed was located. That was about the only cool thing about the place. A bed that actually folded up into the wall was kind of neat. My mom slept on the Murphy bed and I slept on the sofa-sleeper, which was near the window. We didn't have any closets, only two large dressers that were positioned outside of the bathroom. We had one small television that sat atop one of the dressers, but it didn't have cable, so as far as I was concerned, it had limited value.

I went over and laid down on the sofa. I threaded my fingers behind my head and closed my eyes. I blocked out all of the sounds of the city—the wailing fire engine, the loud trunk amps and the sound of multiple conversations. My mind was flashing images of the events that had occurred over the past few months. Directly after the death of my Aunt Estelle and the conviction of my Grandmother Rubylee, my mother was arrested for driving around as a passenger with a friend of hers in a stolen car. While her case was being ironed out, Grandmother Rubylee got in touch with her father's relatives and convinced them to take me in for a little while. I hated living with them because they were mean-spirited people. They treated me like their maid, and if something malfunctioned or got damaged, it was my fault. Even if the utility bill went up, it was my fault. When the charges against my mother were dropped, I was relieved and excited to be back with her. It was clear that things were going to be hard for us, but I figured my mom would step up and make sure we were safe. At least, that was what I was hoping for.

Sometimes I fantasized about who my father was and what it would have been like living with him. I'd never met my father, but in a way, I'd always hoped that he'd magically appear and come and rescue me from my situation. But that was just a dream from the fairy tales of my imagination. I knew someone out in the world was my father, but I didn't know who, and Mother wasn't actually sure, either, or that was what she'd told me over the years. A loud knock at the door startled me back into reality.

"Who is it?" I asked aloud.

"It's me, Toya." *Dang, why doesn't she take a hint?* I thought to myself. *I just want to be alone right now.* I opened the door and she was standing there with her son perched on her hip.

"Girl, I need a real big favor from you," she said. I wasn't in the mood to give out any favors, but before I could tell her that, she unlatched her son, Junior, from her hip and handed him to me.

"I need you to watch him for about an hour," she said. I prepared to hand him back to her.

"Have your grandmother watch him," I said.

"Come on, Keysha, you know that she's going blind and can't see too good. I only left him in the house because he was asleep. I mean, she can watch him but it's not like she's really keeping an eye on him."

"Then why don't you take him with you? He's your son," I said.

"Girl, because I just got a phone call from my cousin telling me that my man is on her block all hugged up with some girl, and I need to go see what's going on with that." There was a long moment of silence between us. I wanted to tell her that she should take her baby with her because I just wasn't in the mood to deal with him right now.

"Come on, girl. I promise I'll only be about an hour." I sighed, and she took my grumbling sound as confirmation that I'd watch him.

"Thank you so much," she said, then left abruptly.

"Don't leave him here all night, Toya. I have to register for school in the morning," I yelled out behind her as she rushed down the corridor and out of the building.

Junior was quiet and didn't say much at all. I could tell that he was in some sort of deep thought. He was about fourteen months old and had beautiful eyes. I sat him down on the sofa and asked if he wanted something to eat.

"I don't have much, but I think I can whip up something that will hold you over for an hour," I said to him. Junior didn't respond. He only stared at me with sad eyes. I knew the sadness in his eyes all too well. I suppose in many ways he and I had something in common—a mother who wasn't ready, or equipped, to be one. I opened up the refrigerator and removed a package of bologna to make a sandwich. *I suppose he can eat this,* I thought to myself, uncertain of what he could and couldn't eat. I fixed him up the perfect sandwich and just as I was about to cut it into smaller portions, I noticed that he'd drifted off to sleep again. *This baby was still asleep when Toya woke him up to bring him over to me,* I thought. I placed the sandwich back in the refrigerator in case he wanted it later on. I went and sat down next to him and situated him so that his head was resting on my lap. I began to stroke his hair and think about what it would have been like if Ronnie and I would've had a baby. I wondered what his or her skin complexion would have been like. I wondered if the baby would've looked like me or him and if we would've made it in spite of all the obstacles that would have been in our way. Ronnie was my first, and I suppose in some ways I'd never forget him. I thought he loved me just as much as I loved him, but I was wrong. Ronnie was only interested in getting down with me and nothing more. It's hard when you don't feel loved. Now that I think about it, that was the reason behind sleeping with Ronnie in the first place. He kept telling me how much he loved me and I believed him. I mean, when a guy tells you that he loves you, he has to be serious about you, right? I mean, I can honestly say I'd never heard my mother tell me she loved me. Sometimes, I just wanted to be hugged. Even though I was a teenager, I still liked to be hugged, but my mother wasn't the hugging type. I felt like I was going to cry when I thought about how empty that part of my heart was. I stood back up and went over to the countertop, which was next to the stove, and retrieved some mail that I'd placed there. I gathered all of my school registration forms, found an ink pen, then sat back down on the sofa and filled out the forms. In many ways, going to school was the only thing that kept me sane. Now how sad is that for a teenage girl? I mean honestly, I didn't know of any girl my age who actually liked going to school.

About two hours later, Toya returned. When she knocked on the door, I was all set to snap out on her for taking so long. I'd gotten irritated trying to keep Junior entertained because he only slept for about forty-five minutes. Keeping his little bad butt entertained was no picnic. When I opened the door, I held my words because patches of her pretty long hair had been ripped out. The T-shirt she was wearing had been ripped and the side of her face and neck had clearly been scratched up.

"What happened to you?" I asked.

"It's a long story. Where is Junior at?" I turned around to call her son to the door but he was already making his way to her side. He gave her leg a bear hug.

"You got into a fight, didn't you?"

"I had to let her know not to sneak around with my guy," Toya said. As I scrutinized her more closely, it appeared that the other girl had got the best of Toya, but I didn't say anything.

"Well, tell me how it went down," I said, wanting to know every detail. I was about to step aside so that she could come in but she wouldn't.

"I don't want to talk about it right now, but I will tell you this. I found out that he has a baby with her, as well."

"Girl, stop lying." I didn't want to believe what I was hearing.

"I'm not—" Toya's voice cracked from all of the emotional energy she was trying to contain.

"I'll talk to you later," she said as she picked up Junior and walked across the hall to her apartment.

It was getting late, and my mother hadn't arrived home yet. When she left earlier that day, she only told me that she was going to take care of some business and would be back. I was hungry, so I pulled out the black skillet from the cupboard along with the rest of the bologna and cheese and fried myself up a sandwich. I loved fried bologna and cheese. I pulled down my mother's Murphy bed and turned on the television before I sat down. I flipped through the channels and finally stopped to watch a rerun of *The Fresh Prince of Bel-Air.*

"Why can't I live like Hillary Banks?" I said aloud. "Have a rich daddy, a goody-two-shoes brother and a crazy cousin who's always doing something that he doesn't have any business doing." The lifestyle that the characters were living seemed so phony and unrealistic to me, but I still enjoyed watching it. During a commercial break, I heard the key enter the lock in the door. A moment later my mom walked into the room. She opened the refrigerator and noticed that the bologna was gone.

"I know you didn't eat all of the damn bologna," she started snapping out on me. Her voice was loud and confrontational, which made me edgy and confrontational, as well.

"I was hungry. What was I supposed to do? Slit my wrists and suck my own blood for food?"

"If it fills you up, that's what you need to do," she shot back sneeringly.

"Whatever," I said, sucking air through my teeth and rolling my eyes at her.

"You better stop rolling your eyes at me before I knock them out of your head." I ignored her violent comment for the moment. She then moved in front of the dresser where the television was and began removing some of her clothes from the top drawer.

"Where are you going?" I asked.

"Out to a club," she answered.

"You know I register for school tomorrow and I still need supplies," I reminded her.

"And?" she replied as if my needs were not her priority.

"I need those school supplies," I answered her back loudly. I hated it when she acted as if I was unimportant.

"Borrow some supplies from a classmate. I don't

have any extra money." She slammed the top dresser drawer closed and then opened up another one.

"But you have money to go to a club," I said, hoping to make her feel guilty about her judgment. She turned and pointed her finger at me.

"Hey, what I do with the money I bring up in this house is my business. I don't have to answer to you for anything! If you want school supplies go get them yourself. I don't have time to deal with you. You're just dead weight on my shoulders, and you're slowing me down. As grown as you are you should be out on your own." Her attitude toward me really hurt, but I wasn't going to let her know. I wasn't about to allow her to get under my skin.

"So you don't care whether I drop out of school or stay in?" I barked at her. I really hated her as a person. At times Justine could be cold, like a pail of ice, and other times she acted as if we were the best of friends. That day, her mood was icy.

"You're only going to drop out and get on public assistance anyway. You didn't get pregnant this time but the next time you will," she said, referring to the time I thought I was pregnant by Ronnie. Thankfully it was a false alarm. "Pregnancy may not be the worst thing for you. At least you'll be able to bring a government check home." Deep inside I was yelling at her and wishing that horrible things would happen to her. Deep inside I wanted the power to strike her down with a bolt of lightning so her feelings would hurt as much as mine. The fact that I didn't have that type of power bothered me. Someday, I'd make her regret the way she treated me. My only wish was for that day to be today.

chapter 3

When I woke up the next morning, my mother hadn't come home from her night at the club. *I swear, sometimes I fear that the police are going to knock on the door and tell me she has been killed or something,* I thought to myself. I knew a long time ago that to a certain degree I'd have to take care of myself early on in life, but at times I really just wanted to be a kid with a normal life. I tossed aside my blanket, placed my feet on the cold floor and then stood up and took a long stretch to begin my day. I went inside the bathroom, took a shower, got dressed and gathered up my school paperwork before heading out the door. When I exited the building, I ran into Toya, who was sitting on the stoop shuffling a deck of cards.

"Where are you headed to?" she asked, glancing at me. Her face still looked pretty bad. Overnight a bruise had formed on her cheek.

"I'm going to register for school. Aren't you coming?" I knew that she wasn't but I thought I'd ask anyway.

"No, I don't have anyone to watch Junior. My grandmother is tripping. She told me to take him with me to registration."

"Why not? I mean, today is only the first day of registration," I reminded her.

"Girl, I have bigger things to deal with than registration and school. I'm trying to figure out when my man had time to have a baby with another girl. Plus my face and hair are jacked-up right now." Toya was quiet for a moment and I didn't say anything. "I mean, she's not even good-looking, Keysha. Her hair isn't as long as mine, her skin looks bad and she has a big gap between her upper front teeth. She pulled out my hair, Keysha. I swear, when I see that girl again, I'm going to cut her with this." Toya reached into her front pants pocket and pulled out a barber's straight razor. "Once I cut her in the face, I'll bet she'll think twice before messing with me."

I wanted to ask the obvious question, which was, "Why isn't she mad with her man for cheating on her?", but Toya didn't think like that. It was never her man's fault. It was always the other woman's fault.

"You'll have to tell me all of the details when I come back," I said, not wanting to listen to her issue at that moment.

"Why are you rushing off? You don't have time for me now? I listened to you yesterday when you talked about breaking up with Ronnie," Toya said, raising her voice at me. I felt guilty for a brief moment and was about to give her a little of my time, but then I glanced up the street and noticed my mother approaching with some guy. He appeared to be some stray man she'd picked up at the club to keep her company.

"Toya, I've got to go. I'll talk to you about this later." I wanted to leave before my mother made me greet her new friend.

"What the hell, Keysha? I thought you were my girl. I thought you cared about what I'm going through."

"I do, Toya, but I've got to get to school. Do you have your enrollment forms? If not I could pick them up for you."

"I told you, I've got better things to do. Why do you care about school, anyway? You're not an A student. You know that you don't want to be there listening to some boring-ass teacher. You'll have more fun sitting here with me all day playing cards. After that we could watch that television program where people get on it and start fighting. I love that show."

"I'm going to have to pass on that today. I don't want to go to late registration. Besides, this is a chance for me to get out of the house. My mother is coming with some weird-looking man." I nodded my head in the direction of my mother. "I'll catch you later," I said and moved past her. I crossed the street to walk down the other side so that I could just wave to my mother and keep on going, but she made me stop and cross back over to where she was. I took in a deep breath and prepared to deal with the nonsense that would fly out of her mouth.

"What's up, girl?" She greeted me as if she were my best friend instead of my mother. I didn't respond right away because I was scrutinizing her outfit. To put it mildly, my mother's outfit was a hot mess. She was too old for the style of clothes she was fond of wearing. She had her oversize behind stuffed into a pair of low hip-riding Phat Farm jeans, which were in desperate need of a belt. She had on a white belly top that exposed her pregnant chocolate tummy, her stretch marks and an old tattoo of a red rose. I'd tried on occasion to help her find clothes that were more appropriate, but she didn't like the fashions I'd picked out.

"I know, girl, I'm fine as wine," she said, mistaking my horrified expression for approval of the way she looked. "I couldn't take two steps without a car honking a horn at me. Isn't that right, Simon?" She looked to her friend to confirm the truthfulness of her statement.

"You know all the men want you, baby," said Simon. The way he was looking at me made me feel as if a thousand bugs were crawling on my skin—honestly, dude made my skin crawl as if I were watching an episode of *Fear Factor*.

"What's your daughter's name again?" asked Simon as he continued to rape me with his eyes.

"Keysha, fool. You know that," my mother answered him.

"Give me a break. I haven't seen this girl since she was a baby," said Simon. He looked over at my mother, and that's when I noticed a hideous scar that ran from his right earlobe, across his cheek and down to the corner of his lip. The site of the scar caught me off guard, and now I was the one doing all the eye raping.

"You don't remember Simon, do you, Keysha?" asked my mom.

"With a face like that how could I ever forget him," I said.

"I got this scar at one of the parties your Grandmother Rubylee used to host years ago. I was helping her collect a debt," Simon said as he continued to stare at me as if he were studying for an exam.

"Simon is an old friend of the family from around the old neighborhood," said my mother. "We used to hang out and party together all the time. We had some good times together, didn't we, Simon?"

"Yeah, we did," he said, smiling at the memory.

"So you two used to date or something?" I asked.

"Something like that." Simon's answer was very vague.

"We ran into each other at the club last night. We got to talking about the old days and the good times. Simon is starting up a business," said my mother. "We're going to go in the house and talk about it."

"Whatever." I rolled my eyes because I didn't care

about what her and Simon were really up to. One thing was for sure, it wasn't about starting a legitimate business.

"Justine, she looks too damn familiar. Who's her father?" Simon smiled at me and his teeth were as yellow as a lemon. I cringed at the sight of them.

"Why do you want to go and ask me a question like that in front of her?" Justine got irritated with Simon.

"You know why I'm asking," said Simon. "She looks just like my cousin—"

"Look—" I cut him off because there was no way I was related to anyone who looked like him.

"Wait a minute, Keysha, let me look at you one more time," Simon said, studying the details of my every feature.

"Take a picture, it lasts longer," I said and rushed away from them.

"Keysha, wait a minute." My mother chased after me.

"What? I'm heading off to register for school," I said.

"Hold on a minute." She grabbed my arm and forced me to stop.

"Why are you just now getting home?" I asked with an authoritative tone. "And why did you bring him with you, and why is he acting like he knows something about me?"

"Who the hell are you snapping at? I don't have to answer to you," she quickly reminded me. At that moment I noticed the unpleasant smell of alcohol and cigarette smoke that was pasted to her skin and clothing. The odor was choking the air between us.

"You need to start acting your own age and not like some teenager who can't control their hormones." I don't know why I said that; it just flew out of my mouth.

"Excuse you!" she barked at me. "Don't mess around and get a beat down in the middle of the street," she threatened me. I didn't say any more because my mother was crazy enough to knuckle-up her fists and fight me right where I stood.

"Why does he think I look like someone he knows? Why does he even think he knows who my father is?"

"Simon doesn't know what he's talking about, baby. He's just talking out of the side of his head. Don't pay him any attention."

"I'll be back later," I said, not wanting to speak with her anymore.

"Hold on a minute." She wiggled her fingers into her front pocket and pulled out a crumpled-up five-dollar bill. "Get yourself something to eat while you're out. I probably won't be home when you get back."

"Why?" I questioned her again. I'd gotten so tired of her being gone all of the time.

"Because I've got things to do. If things work out, I may be able to make a little money today."

"Doing what?" I asked suspiciously.

"I don't know. That's why Simon has come over. He's going to tell me about his business."

I didn't like her answer, and before I could stop my words I found myself interrogating her once again.

"Is it a legitimate job?" She didn't answer me. "Why don't you look for a real job, Mom?" I asked in a softer tone of voice.

"Because I don't have to. That's why I have you, so I can collect a check." She quickly turned icy on me. Her comment made me feel as if I had no emotional value to her. I was just a person she could get a welfare check for.

"You know that the back rent is due, and if you don't pay we could be put out again. I don't think the landlord is playing around."

"I'm not worried about it," she said and didn't offer up any type of comfort to assure me that everything would be okay. I wanted to scream and yell at her. I wanted to explode, but instead I just built a wall around my emotions for her. At the moment I refused to allow her to cripple me emotionally. If she didn't care, then I didn't, either.

"Have fun with your friend Simon," I said as I walked off.

"I will!" she yelled back at me as I rushed off down the street.

I thought for sure the lines for registration would be long, but they weren't. I was able to go through the process fairly quickly. One of the school administrative staff printed out my class schedule and handed it to me.

I glanced down at it and noticed that I had math first thing in the morning.

"Nine o'clock in the morning is too early to have a math class. Can you switch it for me?" I asked the lady who'd printed out my schedule. She looked at me for a long moment, as if I'd lost my mind.

"I guess that means no," I said sarcastically.

She frowned and yelled out, "Next."

My biggest concern now was school supplies or my lack of them. I hated being unprepared but I really didn't have a choice in the matter. I'd have to recycle the folders that I had from last year and latch on to someone when I needed additional supplies. It was an embarrassment I'd have to contend with.

By twelve-thirty that afternoon I'd arrived back home. As I came up the block I saw Toya still hanging around the front of the building toying around with her deck of cards.

"What's up, girl?" I asked as I took a seat on a kitchen chair that Toya had placed on the stoop.

"How are you just going to walk up and take my seat?" Toya tried to sound angry, but I didn't take her seriously.

"My feet hurt from walking in these cheap shoes," I explained as I allowed my fingertips to massage my scalp, which had suddenly started itching. It was a telltale sign that I needed to wash my hair and oil my scalp.

"Do you want me to braid your hair for you?" Toya asked.

"No, I need to wash it before I do anything with it."

"So, how did registration go?" Toya asked.

"It went okay. It went quickly. I have to figure out how I'm going to get my school supplies because my mother—well, you know that I can't depend on her." A mischievous expression formed on Toya's face at that moment.

"You're right, Keysha. We can't depend on our parents because they aren't cut out for the job. What we need to do is look out for each other. Don't you agree?"

"Yeah, I can agree with that," I said as I scratched the dry skin on my left leg.

"Listen, I've been thinking of a way that we can help each other." Toya stopped shuffling her cards and focused all of her attention on me.

"Why are you looking at me like that, Toya?" I asked, sensing she was calculating something in her mind.

"I've got a plan. Junior needs some new clothes and so do you and I. My baby would look so cute in some baby Nikes and some new gear from Sean John. I want some stuff from Phat Farm, and I know that you do, as well. So here is what I say we should do. Let's go down to the mall and get what we need."

"You must have come into some money," I said, joking. She didn't say a word; she just looked at me and forced me to read her thoughts. Toya had a very serious expression on her face.

"You want to go out boosting again, don't you?" I

knew that's what she wanted to do, but I wanted to confirm it.

"Yeah I do." She paused in thought for a moment. "I have got the perfect plan that includes you, me and Junior."

"Toya, you know you're my girl, and I'm all for heading out to the mall for a five-finger discount deal, but why do we have to drag Junior into this? Last time we went out you and I both almost got busted."

"That's exactly why we're bringing Junior with us. He'll act as our decoy," Toya explained, completely convinced that bringing Junior along would work.

"I don't know, Toya." I had a very uneasy feeling about dragging her son along with us. Boosting is not as easy as it sounds. Whenever I go, I'm always on edge because I don't want to get caught.

"Keysha, you know we both need stuff. You need clothes just like I do, and you know that we can make money selling the stuff that we can't fit to the kids at school. You've done this before. Why are you acting as if it's a problem now?"

"I don't know," I answered her as I searched my mind for a reason as to why I was feeling the way I was.

"Listen, we'll put all of the stuff that we get in the bottom of Junior's stroller. If someone tries to stop us, I have a purse full of old receipts that we can use, okay? Trust me, it's going to work. This plan is foolproof."

"How in the world did you come up with that one?"

I asked because Toya's mind was always working a mile a minute.

"I saw someone else do it like that," Toya said, going into more detail. "I went to the grocery store over the weekend for my grandmother. As I was walking past one of the aisles, I saw this woman tearing open a package and stuffing its contents into her baby's diaper bag. Once she was done, I watched her stroll right on out of the store without paying a damn dime. So I thought, *Damn, that's slick, because no one would ever suspect a woman with a baby in a stroller to be out shoplifting.* The security people aren't paying attention to people like her. She was dressed like someone's mother who was just out shopping. The security people are harassing the person who walks in the door looking like a thug. Do you see where I'm going?"

"Yeah," I answered as I began to understand her thinking a little better.

"So all I'm doing is improving on what I've seen. I'll take Junior with me and stuff merchandise into several diaper bags and the compartment at the bottom of the stroller. While I'm doing that, your job will be to distract the sales clerk. Of course, we're going to have to make a few trips to get everything we need, but hey, I think it's worth the effort. Don't you?"

"Yeah, it's worth it," I said even though I still wasn't comfortable with Toya involving Junior in all of this.

chapter 4

We decided to go to Evergreen Plaza, which was on the corner of 95th Street and Western Street. Toya wanted to hit a mall where she was least likely to run into someone she knew. We had to catch two buses and the El train to get there. We had to hop on the Laramie bus and take it to the Lake Street El. Then we took the El to 95th Street. Then we took the 95th Street bus all the way down to Western Avenue. The journey was long and boring until we got on the bus at 95th Street. The bus was very crowded, which meant that some of the passengers had to stand in the aisle. Just as Toya, Junior and I got situated some younger boy dressed like a thug reject tried to step to me. He wasn't cute at all. He had tight nappy hair that needed to be cut, and his breath was so funky I could see the words coming out of his mouth. He had on a dingy white shirt and some baggy shorts that were pulled down so that they could hang low.

"What's up, girl?" He tried to add some bass to his voice but it cracked on him, and Toya and I busted up laughing.

"What's up, boo?" Toya answered as she continued to laugh in his face and bounce Junior up and down on her lap to keep him amused.

"I wasn't talking you. I was talking to your girl, here," he said with a tone of arrogance.

"Oh, well I guess I'll keep my mouth shut, hint, hint…" Toya continued her snickering as she covered her nose with one hand.

"So what's up, girl? Why don't you roll with a baller like me?"

"Maybe if a baller had a breath mint, a hair cut and looked better than you." I laughed.

"Oh, snap!" Toya blurted out. "I think that's your cue to leave, boo."

"I've got a car. It's in the shop right now," he explained, but I didn't want to encourage him.

"Yeah, whatever. You don't even look old enough to drive," I said, thinking that my comment would make him shut up and move on.

"Girl, I just look young. I'm seventeen," he continued.

"Well, you look like you're twelve," I shot back.

"Oh, damn," Toya blurted out once again. "You need to work on your macking skills."

"You know, somebody needs to put that attitude of yours in check," he said as if he were the person who could do it.

"Well, until that person comes along, I would suggest that you leave."

He made a hissing sound and then moved toward the rear of the bus and away from us. "Your ass is ugly, anyway," I heard him mutter. I wanted to say something mean about his mother but decided to let it go. The last thing I wanted was to get into a battle of wits with him. I just wasn't in the mood for it.

"Damn, girl, he was kind of cute," Toya leaned into me and whispered.

"No, he wasn't. That boy looked whack and had breath that smelled like the Crypt Keeper from that show *Tales From the Crypt*. Hell, all he needed was a coffin to complete the look."

"Why are you so mean?" Toya asked as she repositioned Junior on her lap yet again.

"He was on my nerves," I answered as I tried to focus on how we were going to get the merchandise we wanted without getting busted. In the back of my mind, I understood that if I got caught, my mother wouldn't be able to get me out of jail, and I had no one else I could really depend on to rescue me.

"We shouldn't do this today, Toya." I tried to stop her before we entered the mall through the Carson Pirie Scott entrance. My thoughts had gotten the best of me during the remainder of the bus ride down 95th Street.

"No, we're here now, and I didn't sit on that long bus

ride just to turn around and go home empty-handed."
Toya was being stubborn, and I didn't know how to
break through and make her think. I glanced down at
Junior, who was strapped in his stroller fast asleep.

"Keysha, sometimes you have to live for the moment
and do stuff. We can do this and walk out of here with
bags filled with all types of designer clothes." I released
a big sigh as I held the door open for her.

When we entered Carson Pirie Scott, I stopped at the
perfume counter and kept the saleswoman busy with
questions while Toya walked around and removed
several sample bottles from the display counter. Once
she'd gotten what she wanted, she exited the store
through the mall entrance. After I ditched the sales
lady, I caught up with Toya inside the mall.

"Did you get some good stuff?" I asked.

"I got what I could," she answered.

"I'm surprised Junior didn't wake up," I said as I
glanced down at him.

"That's why I was playing with him on the bus, to
make him sleep," Toya said. "I told you. I've thought
about every aspect of my plan. I'm about to go into that
designer store right over there." Toya pointed to where
she was going. I turned in the direction that she pointed.

"Do you see the cashier standing behind the counter
reading a book?"

"Yeah, I see. She's reading *The Coldest Winter Ever*,"
I answered.

"Did you read it?" Toya asked. Toya didn't like reading nearly as much as I did. At times, especially when I'm feeling depressed, I'll go on a reading binge to escape from my reality. *The Coldest Winter* was read during my last escape from my reality.

"Yeah, I read it."

"I knew your ass was a closet geek."

"Shut up. That book was real good," I said.

"Really?" Toya smiled.

"Yeah, I mean, it was good from start to end." I was about to go on and tell her more but she cut me off.

"You can keep her busy talking about the book, while I go in there and rob her blind."

"You just make sure you get me some jeans," I said.

"I got you." Toya winked at me. "Now go in there so that she doesn't think we're together."

I walked into the store and pretended to be shopping for something. The salesgirl didn't even look up at me. I could tell she was lost inside the world the author had created. At that moment, I felt bad that I was about to take advantage of her because I identified with her. I began to think that if she's anything like me, a good book will have her in a daydreamlike state for hours. Sometimes when I read, an entire day can go by without me knowing it. I didn't want to interrupt her reading because when I read, I hate to be interrupted. I glanced back outside toward the mall and saw Toya giving me a strange glare. I could read the expression on her face. She wanted to know why I wasn't talking to the girl. I wanted to tell Toya to hit another store, but I knew she'd have a fit if I suggested it because the setup at this store was too perfect.

"That was a really good book," I mentioned to the salesgirl as I approached the counter. "They should make that book into a movie."

"This would be such a good movie if they made it," said the salesgirl as she glanced up from the page.

"Who do you think could play the roll of Winter?" I asked her. She appeared to be distracted for a moment as she looked past my shoulder toward the front door.

"I'm sorry, I thought that lady over there with the baby needed help."

I turned and looked at Toya, who was reaching down for her diaper bag.

"Are you sure she doesn't need help? I could wait until you're done," I said, taking a huge gamble.

"No, that's okay. She'll probably just look at a few things and leave. That's what most of the young girls pushing a baby do."

"Okay, so if they turned the book into a movie, I think that girl from the television show *The Parkers* should play Winter." I paused as I tried to think of the actress's name. "You know that one that plays Kim Parker, oh, what is her name?"

"Wait a minute, it's coming to me," said the salesgirl.

"She has a weird name, like, Count something." I immediately snapped my fingers.

"Countess Vaughn. That's her name," I finally said.

"I don't know if she could pull it off," said the salesgirl.

"You don't think she could play the part of Winter from the book?" I said, surprised.

"I think you need someone who looks a little harder and rougher. I think Vivica Foxx could play the part."

"She's too old," I quickly pointed out.

"I know, but she could probably pull it off," the salesgirl countered. For the next half hour, the salesgirl and I discussed and debated the character and situations within the novel. I'd gotten so caught up with talking about the book with someone who'd actually read it that I forgot all about meeting back up with Toya. When I finally realized how much time had gone by, I said thank you to the salesgirl and rushed out of the store.

"Hey, what's your name?" she asked before I got out the door.

"Keysha," I said and rushed down the hall before I heard her tell me what her name was. When I caught up with Toya, she had an attitude.

"Dang, Keysha, I just said talk to the girl about the book not have a damn study lecture on it. You'd better watch yourself with all that geek nonsense. You and that girl were talking like the people in that book were real or something."

I wanted to defend myself and tell Toya I really enjoyed reading and it was cool to actually talk to another reader, but she wouldn't have understood. Toya and books just didn't mix on any level.

"Come on, nerd girl. Let's hit another store."

"Don't call me that," I snapped at her.

"All right, bookworm, don't go and get all sensitive on me." I wanted to scream at her for calling me names but instead I kept my mouth shut and followed her down the corridor to the next store. Toya and I hit three more stores and by that time the stroller was loaded down and Junior had awakened and was fighting to be set free from his stroller.

"I think we should head back now," I suggested as we approached the food court.

"Damn, I wanted to hit at least one more store. I haven't gotten Junior anything yet."

"Well, let me go to the bathroom first," I said. We walked into the food court, and Toya took a seat at one of the tables so that she could release Junior from his stroller before he started shouting.

I was about to exit the bathroom but needed to wash my hands first. As I placed my hands under the warm running water, two restaurant employees walked into the restroom laughing and talking loudly.

"Can you believe that dumb girl is down here stealing clothes with her baby?" I overheard one of them say.

"Then she pulled out a bogus receipt talking about how she'd paid for everything." The two girls started laughing uncontrollably. I rushed out of the bathroom and saw that three Chicago Police officers and mall security guards had handcuffed Toya to restrain her.

"Oh, damn," I said as I began to panic. I didn't know what to do. I was frozen with fear. Toya was yelling at one of officers to put Junior down before she filed a lawsuit against them. Toya caught my gaze for a minute and motioned with her head for me to come over to where she was at. I started to take a step towards her but I stopped. I suddenly wanted no part of any of the drama that was going down. To my right there was an exit. Toya must have sensed what I was thinking and so she called out my name.

"Keysha!" she shouted at the top of her voice. As calmly as I could, I turned my back on her and walked hastily toward the exit.

chapter 5

My stomach was doing flips during the entire journey back home. I was nervous, afraid and confused. I placed my elbows on my knees and my face in my hands and tried to think. I wanted to cry but I didn't. I was trying to figure out how Toya got caught. Everything was going so well. We'd moved in and out of stores without any problems. No merchandise alarms went off, and I know Toya was extra careful by making sure she was out of the sight range of the video cameras.

When I arrived home I found a big red notice stuck to our front door. It was an eviction notice. My mom and I had three days to either pay the rent or be set outdoors. *Oh, God, not again,* I thought to myself as I entered the apartment. I walked directly over to my sofa, rested my head on one of the cushions and went to sleep. I woke up in the middle of the night. My mother still hadn't come home, and I needed someone to talk to. The first person who came to mind was my ex-boyfriend, Ronnie. Even though I hadn't spoken to him in a while, I decided to call him hoping he'd be nice to me and listen to my problems. I gathered up some spare change and walked out of the apartment and onto the stoop. When I stepped out into the darkness I noticed that there were people just hanging out. Across the street, there was a group of kids I didn't know listening to music and dancing. To my right, there was a gathering of men sitting on makeshift crates drinking alcohol and talking loudly. To my left, I saw a woman wearing coochie cutter shorts, leaned over into the passenger window of a car talking with two men. Other men who were passing by her on the sidewalk stopped to ogle her behind. At that moment everything in my life seemed to be going wrong. Everyone around me seemed to be crazy, and they were making me crazy just by being around them. I calmed myself down as best as I could and walked up the street to the payphone. I called up Ronnie.

"Yeah," he said as he answered the phone.

"Hey, Ronnie, it's me, Keysha. What are you doing?" I asked.

"Why?" he shot back at me.

"Um…" I lost my nerve for a minute. "Do you really not love me anymore?" I don't know why I asked that question. I suppose in some sort of way I just wanted someone to care about me.

"You know I don't," he answered coldly.

"Do you want to come over? My mother isn't home. We could talk and stuff."

"Naw, I'm not even going to get down with you like that, Keysha. It's over. A baller like me has got to move on."

"You know what, Ronnie, I should come—hello, hello?" Ronnie had hung up on me. I slammed the phone against its cradle and started crying. I let go of my tears for a minute before I got myself together and headed back home.

The following morning, I got up and headed to my first day of school completely unprepared. I walked through the halls dazed and spaced out because I had so much on my mind. I was worried about Toya and Junior and didn't know what to do. I was worried about my mother and how she was going to deal with the eviction notice. I was worried about school because, even though it wasn't socially acceptable to say I enjoyed school on any level other than to socialize, I actually really enjoyed my literature class.

I had no idea of how I was going to make it through school, and the person I depended on would most certainly leave me hanging, just as she'd done so many times in the past.

I just entered my history class and took a seat at the

back of the room. I was hoping the teacher, and everyone else, for that matter, wouldn't notice me. Once the roll call was completed, the course syllabus was handed out. Just as we were about to go over it, the principal and two police officers entered the class room.

"Oh, shit," I whispered loudly. Toya must have tricked on me, and now the police were there to arrest me. I wanted to run out of the room but I couldn't because there was only one way in and one way out. The principal began searching the room, and I scrunched down in my seat as far as I could without actually going up under my desk. I was doing the best that I could to hide in plain sight. The principal finally found the student the police were searching for and I was thankful that it wasn't me.

"Dang, girl, you were trying to get up under the floor," said Lynn Jones, who was one weird girl.

"Yeah, whatever," I said to her.

"What did you do that has you afraid of the police?" she wanted to know.

"None of your damn business," I snapped at her for being nosy.

"Well, forget you, too. The next time the police come into this class I'm just going to start pointing my finger at you so they'll see you."

I leaned over in my seat and looked directly at her. "If you do that I'll put superglue on all of your clothes during gym."

"No, you wouldn't," she said, not believing me.

"Try me," I said, unafraid of her. She didn't say anything else to me so I dropped our conversation.

When I arrived home, I saw Toya's grandmother standing outside the building. She was wearing a one-size-fits-all flower-print dress, some run-over and worn-out looking brown sandals, her black sunglasses for the blind, and she had her white walking stick with the red tip. When I approached her I spoke.

"Hello, Ms. Maze." She turned to the direction of my voice.

"Who is that?"

"It's me, Keysha. Toya's friend," I answered her.

"Oh, how are you doing, baby?" she inquired.

"I'm okay. I'm just coming home from school."

"That's good, honey. I wish Toya was more like you and stayed in school." Ms. Maze hung her head low for a moment. "Oh, I don't know what I'm going to do with that girl."

"Um, where is she at?" I asked because I hadn't heard from or seen Toya.

"She's gotten herself and the baby into some trouble. I'm going to see what I can do about getting her out of jail."

"Oh," I said. I wanted to tell her everything but I couldn't. I just didn't have the courage. "Is she okay?"

"As well as to be expected," she answered me.

"Do you think she'll be getting out today?" I asked.

"I'm going to do my best to get her out," she said.

"Um, where is Junior?" I asked as I shifted my weight from one foot to the other.

"Oh, baby, I don't know." Ms. Maze got choked up and couldn't speak for a long moment.

"Keysha, are you still there?"

"Yeah, I'm here."

"Do me a favor, and stand here with me until the cab I called comes along. I'd like for you to help me get in the car."

"Okay," I said, feeling very bad about her having to go down to the police station to see about Toya. What made me feel even worse was the fact that she didn't know what had happened to her great-grandson, Junior.

When the cab arrived I made sure that she got in without any problem. I then turned to head inside. I was hoping that my mother had come home. When I walked up to our apartment I saw there was another eviction notice posted to the door. I snatched it down and walked inside. The notice said that we now had two days to either pay the rent or be put out.

"Mama!" I called out even though I knew she wasn't home. The Murphy bed was still inside the wall and hadn't been used.

"Damn!" I shouted because I didn't know what to do. I paced back and forth across the floor trying to figure out where she'd gone and where she could be. It wasn't uncommon for my mother to disappear for several days at a time. Especially when we lived with my Grandmother Rubylee and my Aunt Estelle. I really didn't care about her disappearing then because I knew that either Aunt Estelle or Grandmother Rubylee would be around if I needed them. Now our lives were much different, and I had no choice but to worry about where Justine was. I was driving myself crazy trying to figure out what I should do. I finally decided that there wasn't anything I could do. I could only hope that in my hour of need, my mother wouldn't leave me hanging. I could only hope that by some miracle she'd manage to keep a roof over our heads.

chapter 6

When I woke up the following day, I was hoping to discover Justine had come home during the night. To my horror, she hadn't. I swallowed hard and tried not to panic. It was clear that she wasn't going to make it back home. I held on to hope that she'd be home by the time I returned from school, but in the back of my mind and deep in my heart I knew the chances of her returning were slim to none.

I walked over to the bed and got down on my knees. I peeked beneath the mattress and removed a small box filled with photographs. I opened the box and pulled out the first one, which was taken when I was about six years old. My Aunt Estelle took the photo. In the picture I was wearing my favorite blue dress. My hair was combed and braided beautifully. It was Easter Sunday and I was holding a stuffed bunny rabbit and smiling as hard as I could. I remember being so happy that day. It was one of the rare times that everyone was happy. I pulled out another photo of my Grandmother Rubylee and me. I was nine years old in this photo, which was taken at Rainbow Beach. My skin was so brown because I'd been out in the sun all day, and I had brown sand on my legs up to my knees. I was always pretending that my daddy lived in a real castle somewhere very far away and he was waiting for me to come and visit him. When my mother came over to see it, I told her that I thought my daddy lived in a castle like the one I was building. She laughed and said that I had been out in the sun too long and was becoming delusional. She didn't like to talk about anyone being my father. She always told me that she was both my mother and my father.

The final photo was taken at my eighth-grade graduation. I was standing in my blue and silver cap and grown. I'd graduated at the top of the class. I was a straight 4.0 student. I never missed a day of school, did all of my homework and studied hard because I wanted to prove to everyone that I was worth something. I wanted to feel validated in some way. I was so happy that day because I'd made everyone proud of me. It was one of the few times that I can remember where I felt good about myself. That day was perfect, well, at least as perfect as it could have been. Rubylee and my Aunt Estelle were there, but my mother wasn't. Rubylee insisted that she not show up and ruin my day. At the time of my graduation, my mother was in rehab for drug addiction. I remember wanting to do everything that I could to help her stay healthy, but my mother just kept getting into trouble. It was like trouble followed her as if it were a gray storm cloud on a mission to make her as miserable as possible. I didn't work nearly as hard back then. I thought good grades would somehow not only validate me but also motivate my mother to be more supportive and proud of me, but she didn't care at all. I figured, if she didn't care then why should I?

I put the box away because it was depressing me to look through it. I placed it in a bag with my other belongings and left everything sitting on my sofa. I got dressed and headed off to school, even though I really didn't want to be there. But in my mind, it was better than sitting around the apartment worrying myself into sickness. In many ways, school was where I escaped from my reality.

I didn't go directly home after school because I was afraid to. I spent an hour hanging around the basketball court at the park watching shirtless boys shoot baskets. It was cool for a while, but then a gang of girls who were there started making fun of me because of my bad skin and damaged hair, so I left. As I walked home I began to think. If my mother hadn't come home to pay the rent then I knew I'd have to leave, but I didn't know where I'd go. As I approached my building, I saw Toya sitting on the stoop with Junior's father. I was happy to see her, so I rushed up the street calling her name.

"Toya!" I shouted out. Toya gave me a nasty look that made me drop the smile from my face.

"What's going on, wench?"

"Excuse you?" I snapped at her.

"Give me a minute to deal with her," she said to her boyfriend. He glanced at me with judgmental eyes before stepping away to sit in his car, which was parked in the vacant lot near the building.

"Why did you leave me hanging like that?" Toya asked. Her voice was edgy and full of confrontation.

"Toya, I got scared. I didn't know what to do. The police were arresting you. You were yelling and hollering at them. What was I supposed to do?"

"You were supposed to have my back!" Toya pushed my shoulder and I backed up. She wanted to fight me. I could see it in her eyes.

"Toya, look. We just have a big misunderstanding here," I said, trying to calm her down. Other people who were just hanging out on the block started paying attention to our conflict. If we kept up our loud argument, it wouldn't be long before a crowd would form and encourage us to knuckle-up our fists and beat each other senseless for their entertainment.

"No, there is no misunderstanding. All I know is that I should kick your ass for what you did. Because of you, the department of family services took Junior away from me."

"They took Junior from you?" I was surprised by that.

"Yeah, and it's your entire fault," she said, absolutely convinced of her reasoning.

"How is that my fault? I told you not to bring that boy in the first place."

"I called you, Keysha, because I wanted you to come and get him for me. I didn't care about going to jail because I knew I'd get out. But I didn't want Junior to go with me. Instead of helping me, you ran your scary ass out the door."

"You know what—" I stopped backing away from her and stood my ground. "—that is not my fault. I told you that if something went down and we needed to get away, Junior would be a problem. You should have thought about the consequences before taking him along with us. Plus, why are you always blaming other people when things don't go right for you?"

"No. That's not the way I see it." Toya pushed me hard and I pushed her hard back. "Everything that went wrong is your fault. We would have gotten out of there quicker had you not been lollygagging for thirty minutes with that salesgirl."

"Fight!" I heard someone on the street yell out. Before I knew it there were people gathering to watch the outcome of our conflict.

"Toya, let's not do this," I pleaded with her. "We've been friends far too long."

"No, I'm about to open up a can of whup ass on you." Toya reached into a back pocket and pulled out the straight razor she'd shown me a few days earlier. I quickly backed up because I didn't want to end up with a facial scar like my mother's friend Simon. She opened it up and swung it at me but I was too far away from her.

"It wasn't my fault!" I shouted at her, hoping to get her to see my point of view. "Why are you always starting fights?" I asked but didn't get a response. I quickly scanned the ground in search of a weapon of my own but didn't find one.

"Come on, Keysha, you can't run. It's about to go down," she taunted me. I was a nervous wreck. I didn't know what to do. I couldn't turn and run because there was a crowd of people surrounding us; I certainly didn't want to step forward and risk getting split open by a razor.

"Toya, please," I pleaded with her, but she swung at me again. This time she aimed for my face.

"Somebody help me!" I shouted out, but someone from the crowed answered back.

"Help yourself!"

"Toya, how was I supposed to know that was going to happen, huh?" I asked. I figured that if I kept talking I might get through to her. "I mean, why would I want to see them take your baby from you?"

"Because you wanted a baby with Ronnie but you couldn't get pregnant," she snarled back at me.

"That's not true and you know it," I shouted back to her as she swung at me again. That time she almost got me on the neck. The circle of people surrounding us was getting tighter, and I had absolutely nowhere to go.

"If you want to fight then fight me fairly," I said, wanting her to put the razor down. She didn't answer me. We just kept circling each other cautiously, like two angry lions looking for the right moment to strike. She was much closer to me now and swung at me again. I held my hand up to protect my face. The flesh between my thumb and first finger got nicked by the edge of the razor.

"Damn it!" I shouted out as I made a fist to apply pressure in hopes of stopping the bleeding.

"Toya, this is crazy," I said. My voice was shaking with fear. "You've got drama in your life and so do I. I don't have a place to live. The landlord put an eviction notice on my door and today was the last day to pay rent or be put out." Toya suddenly stopped.

"Is that the reason why a strange woman is around asking all types of questions about you and is in your house going through your stuff?" I'd finally gotten through to her.

"What are you talking about? What woman?"

"It serves you right to be put out of the building, because your mother isn't anything but a whore, anyway. She hasn't paid rent because she's in jail. I saw her locked up when I was in jail last night."

"I'm going to give you a pass on that comment about my mother being a whore."

"Y'all are out here faking," I heard someone from the

crowd say. It wasn't long before people started moving away from us.

"Well, it's true. That's why you haven't seen her." I didn't want to believe Toya. I didn't want to believe that my mother had gotten into trouble yet again and left me out in the world to make it on my own. Now that the crowd was gone, I rushed past Toya and into the building. I walked down to the apartment door and found it open. I stepped inside and saw a woman dressed in a black business suit.

"Are you Keysha?" the woman asked but then noticed my bleeding hand. "Are you okay?"

"I'm fine. Who are you and how did you get in here?"

"My name is Maggie. The landlord let me in. I work with the Department of Children and Family Services." There was a long pause as I tried to understand what was going on.

"Your hand is bleeding pretty badly. You should let me take a look at it."

"I'm okay," I said. "Why are you here?"

"Your mother has run into some legal problems and she knew you'd need help. So that's why I'm here, to help."

"Help me do what?" I asked.

"Find a home," she said. I suddenly felt dizzy and light-headed.

"Find a home? It's true, I'm homeless now?" I asked, feeling anxiety, fear and emotional stress attack me all at once.

"There is a group home for teens in your situation that I can place you in."

"A group home." I repeated what she'd said as my vision became gray and blurry. I felt as if my legs could no longer support my weight. I felt them buckling beneath me.

"Sweetie, you're wobbling. Let me take a look at the cut on your hand." I tried to move away from her. I wanted to turn and run out the door, but I fainted instead.

chapter 7

When I regained consciousness, I felt someone placing a cold washcloth around my face and neck.

"Mom, what happened?" I asked.

"You fainted. Your mom isn't here," said Maggie. "And your hand has been cut pretty badly. I called for an ambulance."

"I don't need an ambulance," I said as I tried to sit up, but Maggie placed her hands on my shoulders and held me down. She was a short, bony woman but strong enough to hold me down.

"You need to relax," Maggie reiterated. I didn't feel like struggling with her so I relaxed. I studied her features. She had caramel skin with dark brown freckles around her nose and cheekbones. She was attractive but I could tell by the deep lines beneath her eyes that she'd seen her fair share of heartache, drama and pain.

"Why is everything falling apart?" I started crying

uncontrollably. I wanted Maggie to embrace me and tell me that it was going to be okay but she didn't. I wanted to feel safe, loved and wanted, but all I felt was alone.

When the paramedics arrived, they stitched up the deep cut on my hand and offered to take me to the hospital.

"I don't want to go to the hospital," I said.

"Honey, you really need to have a doctor look at your hand," said Maggie, who seemed to be concerned about me.

"I'm fine," I said as I looked at the bandage on my hand. "See, the bleeding has stopped."

"Will the stitches hold until I can get her to a private doctor?" Maggie asked one of the paramedics.

"Yes," answered one of the men as he began putting away his medical supplies. "But make sure she sees a doctor soon. Don't wait more than one or two days."

"Okay," said Maggie. She thanked them as they walked out of the apartment and down the hall.

Once the paramedics left, Maggie once again asked me how I got cut.

"What do you care?" I snapped at her.

"Okay, I'm just trying to help."

"You don't really want to help me. You're just doing a job," I said as I inspected the bandage around my thumb. She then showed me all of her credentials to prove who she was.

"You can't stay here," Maggie informed me.

"No shit, Sherlock," I said. "I suppose this means

you want me to gather up my bags and go with you." Maggie didn't say anything; she just looked at me. I read her facial expression and deduced that was exactly what she wanted me to do. I walked around the room and gathered up my belongings. I took one last look around the apartment to make sure that I hadn't forgotten anything I wanted.

"What about the television?" Maggie asked. "Do you want to take it?"

"No, it barely works," I answered as I walked out the door. When I stepped out onto the stoop of the building, I thought for sure someone would approach me and ask if I was okay. I mean, I figured that they had to have seen the ambulance and should've known that it was for me. No one looked in my direction or even thought enough about my well-being to ask me what was going on. Toya wasn't around, and I assumed that after she'd cut me, she got in the car with her boyfriend and drove away in case the police were called.

"That's my car over there." Maggie pointed to an emerald-green Oldsmobile. She hit the remote locks and the trunk of the car opened up.

"You can place your bags in the trunk," she said as she moved past me. I took a deep breath and then headed toward her car and my unknown future.

As I drove away with Maggie, I just stared out the car window and didn't say a word. I was angry at everything and with everyone. I was already making plans to run away from the group home. I'd rather take my chances living on the street as opposed to being forced to go into some home with a bunch of people I didn't know. I thought perhaps I could go back and talk with Ms. Maze, Toya's grandmother, and ask her if I could stay with her for a little while. I know the plan sounds crazy after Toya cut me with a straight razor, but I figured we were even now and we could move past that.

"I'm taking you to a facility for distressed teens that is on 114th and Western Avenue," Maggie said, interrupting my thoughts. I didn't want to say anything to her because I didn't like her.

"Has anyone explained to you what has happened?" she asked. I wanted to answer her by saying, "Duh, no one has said a damn word to me," but I didn't. I just gave her the silent treatment.

"Okay, I'll take that as a no answer." She made a right turn and then continued. "There is no easy way to put it so I'm just going to tell you like it is. A few days ago, your mother was arrested as part of a police sting to clean up prostitution in poor neighborhoods. When she was picked up, she had illegal drugs in her possession." I could feel her looking at me, but I continued to look out the window at people who were waiting on the bus. For a brief moment I wondered where they were going, but Maggie continued talking.

"When Justine realized that she wouldn't be getting out

anytime soon, she notified the officials at the jailhouse and informed them of you and your situation. Once it was determined that she was telling the truth, your case was assigned to me. If you allow me to help, we can work together on finding you a good foster home."

I felt as if I'd been kicked in the chest by a horse when she said the words, *foster home*. I never thought I'd end up living in a foster or group home for teens at risk.

"The group home I'm taking you to can be as comforting as you make it. You'll be staying with other teenage girls in a dorm-room setting. You'll be under constant supervision by the adult staff members. The facility works on trying to create an atmosphere of family so that everyone feels comfortable."

"How long do I have to stay there?" I asked with a nasty attitude. I didn't like the sound of the place she was taking me to one bit.

"Well, I'm not sure. I still have to speak with your mother about contacting your father."

"She doesn't know who he is," I said to her. "It could be any one. I could pass him on the street every day and never know it." I paused in thought. "You know her dumb ass is pregnant, don't you?" I tossed out the question because I wanted her to know that my mother suddenly meant very little to me. I had a very low opinion of her. If I saw her on the street, I'd turn and walk the other way. I wouldn't even acknowledge her.

"Yes. I am aware of the pregnancy. That case has

been assigned to me, as well." I didn't say anything else because I was attempting to calm my nerves. I couldn't stop my hand from slapping my knee like a superball bouncing around recklessly. Maggie made a left turn and I noticed that we were going past a bookstore. I would have loved to stop so that I could get a few books to get lost in but I knew that wasn't an option.

"I'm going to be reaching out to a man who may be your biological father," Maggie continued. "She's given me the name of a man who she thinks is your dad."

"Well, how come she's never told me who he is?" I asked.

"Well, according to her, she didn't have a strong sense of who he was until recently. Her friend Simon helped her to narrow down the possibilities."

"Oh, God, please don't tell me I'm related to him."

"I don't know. We'll have to see if this man is willing to be tested. He may refuse testing or deny any type of relationship with your mother." I got so angry that I started slapping the dashboard of the car like I'd gone mad. My emotions were out of control. Maggie didn't say anything. I suppose she was used to sudden emotional outbursts.

"So if this dude takes the test and realizes he's my father then what?" I asked. "Do I get to go live in his castle and live happily ever after?"

"If he does agree to be tested and he learns that you're his child, I'm sure it would have an impact on his life," Maggie said.

"What if I don't want to go with him? What if he's some creep who's just as messed up as my mother? Then what?"

"Well, we'd never put you in a situation where you're in danger of being harmed. If your biological father has a criminal record or is unable to care for you, then you'd be able to remain at the group home until you turn eighteen years old. At that point, you'd be free to go forward and live your life."

"It sounds like a real jacked-up deal," I said as I wiped a tear from my eye. I was trying not to cry.

Maggie pulled into a gas station and turned off the car. She repositioned herself to look directly at me. I refused to make eye contact with her. I continued to look out the window at people who were walking by.

"If you're thinking about running away from the group home let me give you a few things to consider. The streets are very cold at night. You wouldn't know where you'd be sleeping or where your next meal would come from. You run the risk of being attacked or taken advantage of by people who don't have your best interests in mind. All I'm trying to do is help you. If the situation with your biological father doesn't end with 'happily ever after' then you still have the option of finishing your education and even going to college. Hang in there, get your education so that you can locate a good job and support yourself. You seem like a very nice girl who has been dealt a very bad hand, and I'd hate to see you crumble apart. Your situation is bad but I've seen worse," Maggie explained. I still didn't say anything to her.

"Look. All I'm asking is that you stay at the group home if things don't work out for the best."

"It doesn't matter. If this guy is anything like my mother, he doesn't give a rat's ass about me," I said sarcastically. "I don't care what happens to me anymore."

"Be positive, Keysha. Perhaps he will care once he's made aware of your situation." I finally turned and looked her directly in the eyes.

"No one has ever cared about me or loved me, with the exception of my Grandmother Rubylee, who is in jail. I might as well step in front of a bus and kill myself."

"Well, since you feel that way, maybe I shouldn't bother trying to contact this man," Maggie said as she started the motor back up and continued on.

We finally stopped in front of the group home, which was a brown brick bungalow-style structure. The screen door had black burglar bars on it, and the wooden banisters on the front porch needed to be repainted. The brushes around the property were overgrown, and the grass had been completely neglected. All the way at the top of the structure I noticed three small windows, which I assumed was the attic.

Maggie pressed the latch for the trunk and was

about to get out of the car when I stopped her by speaking up.

"Contact him," I said. "Maybe fairy tales do come true."

"Okay," said Maggie.

chapter 8

Maggie took me inside the group home and up to the attic, which had been converted to office space for the adult supervisors. I sat in a chair beside a desk and awaited further instructions. There was one girl who was about my age who was standing at the file cabinet filing. When she saw me she stopped working and glared at me.

"Why don't you take a picture, it lasts longer," I snapped at her. She continued to study me for a moment longer before continuing on with her work. It was noisy in the office. Old-fashioned typewriters were dinging, drawers were constantly being opened and closed and the phone rang constantly. The desks and equipment up there were very old and appeared to be secondhand. The metal desks and filing cabinets were all pea green. The setup reminded me of a police station. The floor plan was wide open, and you could see exactly what everyone was doing.

"Come sit over here," Maggie said, directing me to

another desk. "Once I get you processed, we'll go over some general rules and then I'll give you a tour of the place."

"Rules?" I said. "I'm not following any rules."

"The rules are for your safety. If you break the rules there will be consequences."

"Yeah, whatever," I said, completely unafraid of consequences.

Thirty minutes later, Maggie gave me some basic rules for living in the group home.

"Boys are not allowed in this facility. There is a curfew of 6:00 p.m. on school nights and 7:00 p.m. on Saturday night. If you violate the curfew rule you will be placed in a secured facility. You must treat the staff here with respect. They're here to help and listen to you, as well as help you work through any problems you may be having or going through. Stealing will not be tolerated. Drug usage will not be tolerated. Fighting, inappropriate language or dress will not be tolerated."

"What *can* you do up in here?" I asked.

"Better yourself," Maggie said. I didn't respond to her comment because I wasn't sure exactly how I was supposed to do that.

"It will take me a day or two to get your school records and have them transferred to the high school in this area."

"What? I can't go to my old high school?"

"No. Each morning everyone will get on our school bus, and you'll be driven to school as well as be picked up."

"You're kidding, right?"

"No. I'm not," answered Maggie. "Come on. Let me give you a tour of the place and show you where you'll be sleeping."

The basement of the home had a small cafeteria and a common area with one television, a pool table, a combination bookshelf and magazine rack and three large tables, which were used for studying and doing homework. The main floor was where the sleeping quarters were. Everyone got a thin mattress and one small dresser with two drawers, and that was it. The main floor was also where the showers and bathrooms were located. After Maggie showed me the shower facilities, I followed her to another area where there was a group of lockers.

"This one is yours," she said as she handed me my combination lock. "Don't give your combination to anyone. You can keep your personal hygiene products and any other valuables you may have in here." I opened up the small, rusty locker and was immediately assaulted by an odor.

"Whew," I said aloud as I closed the door.

"I'm sorry about that. I'll have one of the janitors spray some disinfectant in there for you," Maggie said as I followed her back to the sleeping area. "Here is your cot," she said. "I'll let you get settled in. I'm sure the other girls will be along shortly to meet you."

"When are you going to make the phone call to that dude?" I asked. All I had was hope that my biological father was a decent man who wanted a troubled girl like me. I didn't want to stay in here any longer than I had to. In my mind, anyplace was better than where I was.

"I'll do it first thing in the morning," Maggie said.

"Why can't we do it now?" I asked. "I mean, can't you just call him up and say, 'Hey, did you ever have a sexual relationship with a woman named Justine from Chicago?'"

"It's a little more complicated than that. You're in the state system now and certain protocols have to be followed. It's going to take a little time."

"I don't have much time. I want to leave here." I was feeling crazy.

"I'll do everything that I can," Maggie said with a smile and then left.

I plopped down on my cot and placed my face in my hands. Everything seemed so unreal. I just couldn't believe this was happening to me. A short time later, I felt someone nudge the back of my shoulder with their fingertips. I glanced over my shoulder and saw a massive girl towering over me. She had to be at least six foot two and was very heavyset.

"What do you want?" I asked her.

"To look through your bags," she said.

"For what?" I asked placing a very mean expression on my face.

"To see if you have anything that I want." I laughed.

"Honey, if you want to go through my rags to see if anything I have can fit you, then knock yourself out." I stood up and was about to walk away.

"Drugs," she whispered. "Do you have any?"

"No." I glared at her as if she'd lost her mind. Drugs just weren't my thing, especially after watching my mother struggle with addiction.

"They didn't give you any drugs for the cut on your hand? No painkillers or anything?"

"I have to wear the bandage to keep my hand from becoming infected. I don't have any painkillers for it," I said and headed down to the common area. When I got down there, some of the girls were watching an episode of *Jerry Springer.* I went over to the small book-shelf in search of something to read. I felt like escaping from the reality I was in. I didn't want to make friends at that point. I only wanted to be left alone.

The selection of books was very small, and some of the authors I'd never heard of. I picked up three books I thought would be interesting. There was *Lord of the Flies,* by William Golding, *To Kill a Mockingbird* by Harper Lee, and *The Women of Brewster Place* by Gloria Naylor. I picked *The Women of Brewster Place* and went back to my cot. I couldn't wait to mentally check out of the group home by getting lost in a book.

chapter 9

I didn't sleep well at all my first night in the group home. I just couldn't sleep around a bunch of strange people I didn't know or in the strange surroundings. I stayed up most of the night reading. On top of that many of the girls snored loudly. The street lamppost provided just enough light for me to read by. I finally drifted off to sleep at around four o'clock in the morning. At seven o'clock I was awakened abruptly by the sound of someone screaming. When I sat upright, several of the supervisors were trying to restrain the oversize girl who'd asked me if I had any drugs.

"She's coming off of another bad hangover," I overheard one girl whisper to another one.

When they finally got her under control, they searched her belongings and found that she'd somehow gotten hold of some alcohol.

"That heifer is crazy," I heard yet another girl in the room say.

Once the supervisors found what she'd taken, they escorted her out of the dorm room. The other girls just sat and watched the whole thing go down without saying much more. It was strange watching all of this unfold. It was like being in a movie for the mentally ill. I felt as if I was watching things happen but not actually a part of it. In some ways the dorm room filled with cots felt like a ward at an insane asylum. Perhaps we were all just too emotionally empty to react to the madness that was going on around us. Perhaps we just couldn't cry or talk about our pain anymore. Whatever our reasons, none of us moved an inch as the girl was being removed.

Later, after everyone had gone to school, I took a long shower, got dressed and hung out in the common area. I was waiting on Maggie to arrive with my transcript so I could get registered at a new high school as well as take me to the doctor to have my hand examined. I picked up an old issue of *Vibe* magazine that was lying around and started reading an article on Usher. *God, if I had a boyfriend as fine and as rich as him, I'd be set*, I thought to myself. I'd just finished reading the article when I heard Maggie calling out my name.

"Oh, there you are," she said with a monotone voice. "Are you ready?"

"Yeah, I suppose," I said as I stood up and followed her. Maggie got me registered and I started school on the same day. *At least she thought enough to get me a book bag and plenty of supplies,* I thought to myself. I didn't know what my future held but there was no sense in worrying about what I couldn't control.

Several weeks went by, and I hadn't seen or heard from Maggie. I thought she'd left me hanging just like everyone else. I didn't make any waves, nor did I consider any of the girls to be my friend. At this point they were only acquaintances. I had a few conversations with some of the girls, and we even shared a few laughs but nothing real meaningful developed after that.

The adult supervisors had therapy sessions that they encouraged everyone to participate in. A group of us would form a circle and openly talk about our problems. Sometimes I participated and other times I didn't. It was depressing to sit and hear details about the situations some of the other girls came out of. Some were drug users, some were homeless teens from different states and others were selling themselves on the streets in order to buy food or purchase a bus ticket to a new town. It was sad, and downright horrifying listening to stories of sleeping in abandoned warehouses with rats and begging for money on the street corner. One girl named Africa, who was the same age as I was, talked about how she'd stand on the street corner and sing for money to get food. Her parents came to the United States from Haiti, but they both died in a fire when she was twelve. She was placed in a foster home but was abused by her foster mother, so she ran away. While living on the streets she had to constantly fight off men who tried to attack her while she slept on a mattress with a sickly stray dog she was trying to take care of.

"I named my dog Port-Au-Prince, which is where my family is from. He protected me during those times. No matter how sick he was feeling, he wouldn't let anyone get too close to me. He would always bark, even when it hurt to do so."

"What happened to Port-Au-Prince?" I asked her. Before she could answer, she started crying. "I was singing on a corner one morning trying to get enough money to buy him some food. He was lying down beside me, and when I'd finally gotten enough money I called to him, but he didn't move. He died while I was singing."

"What song were you singing?" asked another girl.

"An old song by Sam Cooke called 'A Change Is Gonna Come.' My mother loved that song." Africa sang for the group, and by the time she was done I was in tears. One thing is for sure, I didn't want any part of what I heard had happened to her to happen to me.

Early one Saturday morning, the group was scheduled to go for a fall outing to a local theater to watch a stage play. I had just boarded the group van but was pulled off of it by Maggie. I hadn't seen her in weeks.

I followed her back inside and upstairs to the office where we'd be able to speak privately.

"I really wanted to go see that stage play, Maggie," I said to her.

"Well, we have to do something else instead. I have to get you over to a doctor for a blood sample."

"Blood sample for what?" I asked.

"I got in contact with the man that your mother said might be your dad. At first he said that he didn't recall who your mother was and that there was a mix-up," she explained. "I didn't hear from him for a few weeks and then, out of the clear blue sky, he called me back."

"Well, what did he say?" I asked, holding my breath on her every word.

"Apparently he has a cousin named Simon."

"The man that my mother got caught up with?"

"Yes."

"Oh, great. If my biological father is related to Simon, you can forget it. I'll just stay here at the group home."

"Well, hang on before you say that. Simon and the man who may be your father are as different as night and day."

"Go on, I'm listening," I said.

"Simon got in contact with his cousin through another family member and reminded him about a particular house party they'd gone to years ago when they were both young men. An encounter occurred between Simon's cousin and your mother."

"But Justine doesn't remember this, right?" I asked.

"I don't know what your mom remembers. Anyway, I got a phone call back from Simon's cousin and he has agreed to be tested just to make sure he doesn't have any children out in the world he's not aware of." I swallowed hard. I felt my heart racing and I couldn't calm myself down.

"So, we're going to head over to the clinic for a blood sample and let science tell us if we've located your biological father." I exhaled loudly. My feelings were somewhere between happy and terrified.

"I know this isn't easy," Maggie said.

"I'm afraid," I admitted as I swallowed hard.

Several weeks after my blood sample was taken, Maggie resurfaced again. I was in the common area playing Monopoly with Africa and a few other girls when Maggie rushed in and called out my name, "Keysha." I could hear the excitement in her voice. I captured her gaze.

"Come on, let's go upstairs into the office." I excused myself from the table and followed her. The upstairs office was as busy as it always is. The phones were ringing, the typewriters were dinging and there was a continuous hum of several conversations taking place at the same time. I took a seat in front of the desk where Maggie sat.

"The test results came back."

"And?" I asked, fearing the worst.

"We've found him," she said with a smile. I couldn't believe it. I suppose I should have been happy but I was actually mortified by this new information.

"Well, aren't you happy?" she asked.

"I don't know. I mean, who is he? What is he like? Does he even care about me?"

"His name is Jordan, and he's doing very well. He's married and has a son who is a few years younger than you." She paused in thought for a moment. "He and his wife have agreed to come and meet you."

"Come and meet me?" I began to feel a panic attack setting in. "How about coming to get me the hell up out of here?"

"Keysha, don't get upset. I mean, your existence is very shocking and unnerving to him. This has changed everything for him. He never knew about you."

"Well, he does now, and I don't understand why he just doesn't come down here and pick me up so that I can go!" I was emotional and shouting at Maggie. I didn't mean to shout at her but my emotions weren't in full control.

"Keysha, you have to understand the situation he's in, too. He had to explain you to his wife and the rest of his family. I mean, give him credit, he was man enough to admit he'd had an encounter with your mother. He and his family have yet to make a decision on what to do."

"Well, I'm part of his family. What about what I have to say?"

"Calm down, okay?" Maggie said, trying to get me to relax.

"Okay, I'm cool. When will they be here?"

"In a few days. His mother is coming into town, and he wants to wait until she arrives before he comes because she wants to meet you, as well."

"Well, what's his name?" I asked again.

"His name is Jordan," Maggie said. For a moment I felt good about knowing his name, but then random thoughts began dancing around in my head.

"What if they don't like me? What if they don't want me? What if—"

"Slow down, Keysha. Be patient. There are a lot of things that are still unclear, okay?"

"I can't be calm," I said, feeling my nerves buzzing.

"Keysha, whatever the outcome of all this is we're going to do what is best for you." Maggie smiled at me warmly. I didn't say anything else. I just tried to maintain my composure and hope that my father was the type of man who would understand me as well as get along with me.

chapter 10

On the day I was scheduled to meet my biological father for the first time I was a nervous wreck. I wanted to look my best for him. I wanted to look perfect for him, but the clothes I owned made it impossible to look perfect. My hair was in horrible shape, my skin was full of pimples and I just felt completely inadequate. I was all set to just forego the meeting, but Maggie insisted that I at least meet him.

By 11:30 a.m. I was sitting in the office on one of the chairs awaiting their arrival. Finally, after waiting what seemed like an eternity, Jordan, his wife and his mother finally entered the room, and I was stunned into silence. They all looked so well and healthy. Jordan was impeccably dressed. Everything about him looked expensive, and I began to think that there had to be some type of mistake because there is no way that a man who looked like him would ever be involved with my mother or Simon. He was very handsome; he had smooth brown skin and eyebrows shaped exactly like my own. He didn't have any facial hair, and although his eyes appeared to be closed, I could tell that he was watching me and his vision was as sharp as a hawk's. Sometimes I hated my ability to read a person's thoughts through their facial expressions. My father did not look very enthused about being there. I stopped reading his mind and focused on his clothes again. He had on a gray pin-striped business suit with a very nice yellow satin shirt and matching tie. He had a gold watch on that was bling-blinging all over the place and some very expen-sive-looking shoes. My other grandmother looked very regal. She was tall and full-figured and had on a beau-tiful dress that flowed well with her body. Her hair was styled nicely and had beautiful streaks of gray running through it. She looked as wise as she was beautiful. When I looked into her eyes I could see pain in them. As I studied the two of them, I saw another part of myself that I hadn't known and for some reason I felt cheated. In my heart I knew we were connected, but in reality our relationship was estranged. Then there was Jordan's wife, Barbara. She walked into the room with her nose wrinkled up as if she smelled a foul odor. Ev-erything about her—from the way she was dressed to her demeanor—said uptight, confrontational and mean-spirited.

"Come here, baby." My other grandmother sum-moned me to her once we made eye contact. I took a deep breath, stood up and walked over to her. She embraced me tightly and for a brief moment, the warmth of her hug felt beautiful and I got lost in the sweet scent of her perfume, but I didn't hug her back. I didn't know her like that.

"My name is Katie," she said, smiling at me. "I'm your grandmother." I looked into her eyes and somehow I felt as if she could see right through me. I wanted to say something but my words got trapped in my throat. These new feelings were foreign to me. I was looking into her eyes and felt like I knew her, but I didn't. I looked over at Jordan, and my heart started beating so fast that I thought it was going to smash through my chest.

"Hello. My name is Jordan," he said with a very commanding voice that made me nervous. Just hearing such a strong and unyielding voice made me swallow hard. We stared at each other for a long moment. Then without even thinking about it we both said, "You're reading my thoughts through my facial expressions." It was the weirdest thing that has ever happened to me. We had never known each other, but we knew each other in this bizarre way.

"It's okay. We're going to get you out of here," said Grandmother Katie. I backed away from my father because I didn't fully trust him. He was a total stranger, and yet he wasn't.

"Hello," I finally greeted him begrudgingly. I don't know why I had an attitude toward him.

"Are you okay?" he asked, trying to sound concerned, but I didn't truly think that he was.

"Does it look like I'm okay?" My tone of voice was filled with snake venom. Our eyes locked on each other again; he was trying to understand me just as much as I was him.

"Keysha, come here." Grandmother Katie once again summoned me to her side. "I know how you must feel but things are going to change, I promise," she said. I was so nervous at that moment I felt the urge to pee. I took a deep breath and began biting my fingernails.

"Hello, I'm Maggie Russo. I'm Keysha's social worker," Maggie greeted Jordan's wife, who looked like someone had just stolen her million-dollar lottery ticket.

"How did this happen?" Barbara asked Maggie. "We never knew about her."

"Jordan, if you, your mother and your wife would come over here we can discuss this situation a little more privately. Keysha, would you please have a seat over there in the manager's office." Maggie directed me to a small office that was just on the other side of the wall. I exhaled loudly and stomped over to a seat and made more noise than I needed to. I didn't go inside of the office right away. I hovered near the door where I could still hear their conversation. I listened to them talk about my case.

"Jordan, you can't deny that girl if you wanted to. She looks just like you," I heard Grandmother Katie say. "I know that you didn't know about her, but now you do. You can't leave her in this situation. She's your flesh and blood."

"Mom, please." Jordan wanted his mother to be silent for a moment. "I have a family," I heard him say. "I can't just move her in and make everything work."

"Can't you find a nice foster home for her?" I heard Barbara ask.

"At her age, it would be difficult for us to place her in a foster home."

"She has problems, right?" I heard Barbara ask another question.

"Problems that are not her fault," I heard Grandmother Katie argue back.

"Let me interrupt you guys for a moment," said Maggie. "Right now, Keysha is hurting emotionally. She's been through a lot, but she's nowhere near as bad as some of the other cases I'm dealing with. She's not pregnant, she still enjoys going to school and she's drug free. I have kids younger than her who are pregnant, drug abusers and prostitutes. Many of them have been assaulted as young children and have self-esteem issues that you couldn't possibly imagine. In my heart, I know Keysha is a good kid. What she needs right now is a good, stable home with a lot of love and attention. Now, Jordan, biologically she is your daughter and responsibility. The state is overburdened, and a lot of kids fall through the cracks. However, it is understandable how this can be very disruptive to your current family. You have two options. You can agree to take your daughter with you, or you can sign over your parental rights and let her continue living here until she turns eighteen."

"What happens to her then?" Jordan asked.

"It's hard to tell. We do offer some assistance with college or job training, but it's a very hard road and only a small percentage of the kids actually make it. A lot of them end up falling into a life of crime or some sort of addiction."

"What about her mother? Did she sign over parental rights?" asked his wife.

"She automatically lost them once she was placed in jail," Maggie answered her.

"Will she get her parental rights back once she gets out of jail?" I heard my father ask. I felt so worthless when I heard him ask that question. I felt like he didn't see me as a part of him. I went into the office and sat down because I didn't want to hear any more of what he had to say, because I knew that in the end he'd leave me hanging just like my mother had.

About an hour later, Grandmother Katie came over and sat next to me. She draped her arm over my shoulder and hugged me once again.

"This is all going to work out," she reassured me but I didn't believe her words. "We're going to get you out of here. It's just going to take a little time though."

"You're kidding me, right!" I blew up because I figured it was all just a big lie. "You know what. He doesn't want me! You don't want me! His wife doesn't want me and neither does the state! Nobody wants me so I might as well just go and kill myself to make it easier on everyone!" I yelled at the top of my voice. When I quieted down, the entire staff was glaring at me through the office door, stunned into silence. I couldn't take the pressure so I ran out of the office and back to the sleeping area. I lay facedown on the cot and cried out loud into my pillow.

chapter 11

The following day, Maggie told me she would be meeting with my mother to discuss what the best options would be for the unborn baby she was going to have while still in jail. I told her I wanted to go with her because I wanted to see her. I had questions I wanted to ask her. When we arrived at the jailhouse it was scary. There were metal detectors and armed guards everywhere. We had to take off anything metal that we had on before going through the detector. Even after going through the detector, I had to be patted down to make certain that I wasn't sneaking in anything that I shouldn't be.

I went into a room with Maggie and sat at a long table that had partitions on each side for privacy. In front of me was a thick sheet of bulletproof glass and a black telephone. On the other side of the glass was an empty chair with the same setup. I had to wait for a long time before the guard brought Justine out. When

I saw her, I was actually happy to see her, even though the circumstances weren't the best. I picked up the phone at the same time she did.

"Hey, Mommy," I said, noticing how tightly her hair had been French braided. I couldn't help the way I felt at that moment. My feelings were trapped somewhere between angry and uncertain.

"What's going on?" Justine asked.

"Nothing. I mean, a lot. Things are so chaotic right now. I'm living in a group home for teens and the other kids in there seem real crazy."

"Did that social worker get in touch with the man who might be your daddy?" Justine seemed to be indifferent about whether I found out the identity of my father. I think she was sensitive about the fact she really didn't know who he was after all of these years.

"Yes," I answered her.

"Did he come down to see about you?" she asked.

"Yes," I answered again.

"I didn't think he'd really show up after all this time, but Simon said he would." She paused in thought. "Well that's the best that I can do for you right now. Hopefully he'll take you in."

"I wouldn't count on it," I said, feeling my anger swelling up. "He doesn't want me."

"Well, neither did I, but you're here." Those words hit me like a wrecking ball slamming against a structure being demolished. I wanted to holler at her but I didn't. My heart just iced over and I realized that coming to see her wasn't such a good idea.

"You have to make it on your own," she told me. "I can't do anything more for you. You're old enough now to make your own choices. Hopefully, you'll make some good ones so that when I get out of here I can come and stay with you." What was that supposed to mean? I mean, damn! I can hardly take care of myself, and she's telling me to start preparing to take care of her. At that moment, I wanted nothing more to do with her. At that moment, I heard a little voice in the back of my mind telling me I was worthless and should disappear off the face of the earth because no one cared about me.

"Well, that's all I have to say," she informed me and then hung up the phone. I looked at her one last time and tried to read her thoughts but I couldn't. I got up and left the room. Maggie, who was waiting for her turn to speak with my mother, didn't say anything to me. I suppose the look on my face said it all. She went into the bulletproof room to speak with my mother without saying a word to me.

Three weeks had gone by since I'd seen Grandmother Katie and my father, Jordan. Just like always, I figured they had left me hanging and had no intention of coming to my rescue. I didn't expect them to return at all because, as I heard his wife put it, "I've got problems." Hell, in my mind, we've all got problems.

I was having a very difficult time concentrating on my schoolwork. I couldn't focus, especially after being rejected by my biological father and mother. I just didn't care about much of anything anymore. I didn't care about school, my grades, or the people at the group home or anyone, even myself. The only thing that kept me from going nuts was books.

One day when I was feeling particularly low and depressed, Africa came over to my bed and sat by me.

"You don't look so hot," she said.

"Things are just real jacked-up for me right now. My life isn't worth living," I said.

"Sure it is," Africa said, trying to reassure me, but her words were of no comfort. "I know what it is like to feel the way you do."

"No, you don't," I snapped at her.

"Yes, I do," she snapped right back. "You look as if you want to just give up on everything." I didn't say anything.

"Yeah, that's what I thought. I've been there several times but I never had the nerve to go through with it. I guess I was too afraid to take my own life."

"So what kept you going?" I asked.

"I don't know. I just took one day at time. Some days were better than others, but I always knew that I'd find a way to make it through my problems."

"Don't you want to get out of this place? Don't you want to live with a family again?" I asked.

"Listen, when I was fourteen I joined this all-girl gang. For a while they served as my family, but the things we were doing—well, let's just say I have plenty of regrets about it. I barely made it out of the gang alive, but I did, and I'm thankful for that. Yes, I do want to get out of this place, but not right now. It's safe for me here, and it's much better than living on the street." I didn't say anything else.

"Hang in there. It will get better. It has to," said Africa, who then got up and left. It was thoughtful of Africa to try and cheer me up, but it didn't help because I still felt all alone. Maggie told me I should keep a diary of my feelings and share them in group, but I wasn't really sure how to do that. All I knew was I was hurting really bad and I wanted my mother and father to know how much I hurt.

During our Saturday trip to the library I came across a book called *The Diary of a Young Girl* by Anne Frank. At first I didn't think I'd like reading some white girl's diary, but for some odd reason I sat down at a table with it. I opened the book and started reading it and got pulled into the story. I checked the book out and went back to the group home. I sat on my cot the rest of the day and read. I cared about Anne in a way that I have never cared before, and when I reached the end of the book, I cried for her. After reading what she'd gone through I decided that my life wasn't as bad as it could be. I mean, at least I didn't have to hide from soldiers inside a dark room and remain motionless and silent for hours on end just to save my life. I also didn't have to live on the streets like Africa had to.

The following Saturday evening, I was sitting on my cot reading another copy of *Vibe*. This time I was reading an article about how Beyoncé Knowles got her start in show business. Just as the article was getting good, I heard Grandmother Katie call my name. I looked up and saw her approaching me, wheeling a small suitcase behind her. Jordan and Maggie were with her.

"Let's start packing your things You're not staying here another night," said Grandmother Katie.

"What's going on?" I asked, confused.

"You're going to come live with me," said Jordan.

"What if I don't want to live with you?" I was being defiant.

"No, you're coming to stay with me. You have no idea of what it took to make this happen." Jordan spoke as if I had no real choice in the matter. He was serious, but I was suspicious. Inside I really wanted to be happy, but I wasn't. Since I'd given up hope that anyone was coming for me, I'd gotten sort of comfortable living in the group home. Now I felt as if I were being uprooted once again and being carted off into the unknown.

"And you have no idea of what I had to go through just being here." My words were full of pain and contempt for him. I felt like fighting him, but I didn't know why.

"There is no need to be nasty with me. I'm your father and I want to help."

"Oh, now you want to be my father." Now I was really ready to fight. I'd shifted my body weight from one foot to the other and was about to unleash a verbal assault on him.

"Come on, now," Grandmother Katie's soothing voice cut the tension between us. "Now is not the time to have this conversation. Keysha, come with us. There is so much that needs to be said and understood. Now is the time for healing your bruised heart. It is not the time to create more wounds with angry words."

Grandmother Katie was good. She was very skillful in the way she defused the tension between Jordan and me. For the moment, I decided not to fight with him.

"Come on, start packing your belongings," Jordan said to me in a nicer tone of voice. *Here I go again,* I thought to myself. *I wonder what my life is going to be like now.*

chapter 12

I said goodbye to Africa and a few other girls that I'd gotten to know. We promised to keep in touch with each other, and I promised Africa that as soon as I got settled in I'd call her. We hugged each other for a long moment before I finally departed with Jordan.

During the long drive to my father's house, Grandmother Katie began asking me questions about my mother and our lifestyle.

"Has your mother ever held a job?" she asked.

"No, not one that I can think of."

"Have you been in touch with your other grandmother?"

"No," I answered her.

"What exactly happened to her? I know that she was mixed up in some type of mess with a bank, or at least that's what I've been told." I didn't want to talk about my Grandmother Rubylee. I missed her, and it was still difficult for me to talk about it because it made me think about my Aunt Estelle and how she passed away.

"Can we not talk about this right now?" I asked.

"Okay," said Grandmother Katie. "I understand. We can talk about it later." I remained silent for a long while as we drove down the highway. My father didn't say much but I could tell that he had a lot on his mind. I suppose we are alike in that sense. Whenever there is something eating away at us, we prefer to remain silent and think about the situation before talking about it. I know that my thoughts were all over the place. I was fearful, uncertain and confused. I felt like I was being forced on my father, and that made me feel as if I was some germ no one could get rid of.

"We have enough room for you," said Jordan, who only began speaking after I saw Grandmother Katie nudge him. "You also have a brother. His name is Mike."

"You'll be in the upstairs bedroom down the hall from him. He's a bit apprehensive about your coming to live with us. He's been the only kid in the house for a long time, and he now has to learn how to share." I didn't know what to say so I remained silent.

"I know you'll find living with me to be a lot different, but I know that it's for the best."

Whatever, I thought to myself. In the back of my mind, I was already thinking about running away. To where, I don't know. I just wanted to be alone and not be bothered.

* * *

We turned into this community where there was nothing but beautiful green grass and large homes. I took in everything. I saw both black and white people out mowing their lawns and planting flowers. A few younger kids were riding their bikes along the sidewalk. We finally turned into a driveway and I focused on the house.

"Here we are," said Jordan as he drove down a long driveway. My jaw dropped when I saw the home.

"This is where you live?" I wanted to be sure I wasn't dreaming.

"Yes, and now you'll be living here," said Jordan. The house was two stories tall. It was a soft shade of green with red roof shingles. The underground sprinklers were on. I noticed that there was a greenhouse attached to it that appeared to be filled with all types of flowers that were bursting with color. Once we reached the end of the driveway there was a large black iron gate. Jordon touched a remote that was in the car and the gates opened up. We drove in, and he parked the car in front of one of the doors of the five-car garage.

"Okay, we're here," Jordan said once again as he glanced into the rearview mirror to look at me.

"Do you like it?" he asked with a slight smile.

"It's all right," I said, not wanting to give him the satisfaction of knowing that I was completely impressed.

"It's just all right?" he asked again.

"Yeah, it's just all right," I answered him back.

"Jordan, why don't you give her a tour. I'll take her things up to her room and meet you guys up there," said Grandmother Katie.

"Is it okay with you if we take a walk around the property, Keysha?" asked Jordan.

"I guess it's not like I have a choice," I answered sarcastically.

We got out of the car and stepped into the bright sunlight. I heard a chorus of birds singing, and for the first time noticed all of the trees that surrounded the house. I counted a total of eight.

"This is the garage," Jordan said as he opened one of the bay doors. We stepped inside. The garage was bigger than the apartment I lived in with my mother. Everything inside was organized and in its proper place. Items like bicycles, the lawn mower, leaf blower and hedge trimmer hung from hooks in the ceiling. There was plenty of shelf space and plastic color-coded and labeled containers on each shelf. To my right I noticed a car covered with a black cloth. Jordan noticed me staring at it.

"Do you want to see what kind of car it is?" he asked. Before I could answer he walked over to it and removed the covering. Beneath the cloth was a black sports car with an eagle painted on the hood.

"This is my 1979 Pontiac Trans Am," he said proudly. "I've spent a small fortune rebuilding it to its original condition."

"Do you ever drive it?" I asked. He looked at me strangely as if the thought of pulling it out of the safety of the garage would take an act of God.

"Rarely. This car is a classic. I drive it each year in the Memorial Day parade but that's about it." I looked around the garage a little more closely and saw that there was an additional door.

"What's in there?" I asked.

"Go ahead and take a look," he said. "I'll be along once I finish re-covering the car. I don't like dust getting on it." When he said that I quickly realized that his old car meant a great deal to him. I walked over to the other door and opened it up. Inside was a small workshop. It was tidy and well organized. On the shelves were various containers of paint, wood stain, tools and other items used for building and repairing.

"This is my workshop," Jordan said as he entered the room.

"You build stuff?" I asked.

"I restore things," he said. "Have you ever heard of the phrase, 'one man's trash is another man's treasure'?"

"No, I've never heard of the expression," I lied to him. I don't know why I did. I just did.

"It means that what one person tosses away, another person may find value in."

"Was the old-time car someone's trash?" I asked.

"Yes, it was. The man who had it sold it to me for

only a few hundred dollars. It was just sitting on his property rusting away. I had it towed here and over the course of about seven years I rebuilt it." I was impressed but I didn't let him know it.

"So what do you build in here?" I asked.

"I restore furniture that I buy at garage sales."

"You're basically like the junk man who rides around in a raggedy pickup truck picking up everyone's junk on the street," I said as I found a way to identify with what he did. I could tell that he didn't like my comparison because he didn't respond to my comment. I wanted to laugh at him for being so sensitive but I didn't. "Where do those stairs lead to?" I pointed toward the back of the room.

"Come on, I'll show you," he said. I followed him through the work area and up the back staircase. When we got upstairs I was speechless at what I saw.

"This is the apartment above the garage. I had it converted to a workout gym," Jordan said as he flipped a few light switches so that I could take a better look. There were a number of machines positioned all around the room. There was a flat-screen television mounted on the far wall, and two treadmills were situated in front of the television.

"Do you know who this is?" he asked pointing to a mural on the wall. The wall painting was a life-size portrayal of two boxers. One had knocked the other one down and appeared to be towering above him yelling down at the other man on his back.

"That's that boxer man," I said, not remembering his name.

"His name is Muhammad Ali. He's fighting a man by the name of Sonny Liston. In this scene, Ali has knocked Liston down. Liston was the heavyweight champion at the time. Ali is yelling 'get up' to him."

"Why is he yelling at him?" I asked.

"Because Liston knew that he couldn't beat Ali so he tried to cheat by placing an eye irritant on his boxing gloves. So every time he hit Ali near his eyes, the irritation prevented Ali from seeing clearly. Once Ali's trainers realized what was going on, they washed the irritant away and Ali went back out to whip Sonny's behind."

"Oh," I said as I walked up closer to the mural. "Who painted it?"

"Your uncle did," Jordan answered. I looked back at him and noticed that he was just watching my every movement. His sharp eyes made me nervous. He made me feel as if he was mall security or someone watching and waiting for me to steal something.

"Don't stand behind me like that," I said, snapping at him.

"Stand behind you like what?" he asked.

"Like you're waiting for me to break or steal something."

"I'm sorry. I don't mean to make you feel that way," he said.

Next to the Muhammad Ali painting was a cabinet filled with track and field trophies.

"Did you win these?" I asked.

"No, actually most of them belong to my wife, Barbara. She was an exceptional high school and college track and field athlete. The three on the bottom shelf belong to your brother, Mike."

"Where is he?" I asked.

"He's out with his mother. They'll be home in a little while. You'll see him then."

I got tired of looking at the workout room and decided to walk back down the stairs.

"Come around this way," Jordan said, and I followed him around the side of the garage down a short brick path, which was lined with thick, neatly trimmed bushes. Once we got around the bushes I saw the in-ground swimming pool.

"Do you know how to swim?" he asked.

"No," I answered.

"Well, I can teach you how. It's real easy once you get the hang of it." I didn't answer him, I just looked at how pretty the water was. "We'll have to wait until next summer for swimming lessons though. I'm going to have to drain the pool for the winter next week."

We walked back down the short brick path past the garage and to the door at the rear of the house. I stepped inside and held the door open for Jordan. Upon entering he began talking.

"We'll start in the basement," he said and I followed him down a few steps. To the right there was a door, which he opened. It was his office. His computer, desk and photos of various entertainers were hung on the wall. I walked in and looked at one photo of him and TuPac.

"You knew TuPac?" I asked.

"I wouldn't say that I knew him but we've met before," answered Jordan.

"So what is that you do?" I asked.

"I'm the executive vice president for Hot Jamz 104," he answered.

"That's, like, the hottest radio station in the city," I said, sort of excited about the possibility of getting to meet a famous entertainer.

"Yeah, but our last rating has us as the number-three station in the city and I have to change that."

"Oh," I answered, not fully understanding what he meant. We came out of the office and went toward the rear of the basement. It was a typical basement. Gray concrete floor and walls. There was nothing exciting about looking at the laundry shoot or the washer and dryer.

"Over here, this is what I wanted to show you," he said as he opened another door, which led to the greenhouse. I stepped inside and saw an array of potted flowers blooming along with another door which led inside.

"It's pretty," I admitted and then turned and exited the room. I could tell that Jordan wanted to explain all of the flowers but I didn't care about that.

"I planted all of the flowers around the house," he commented as we walked out of the basement. "Gardening is something I've always loved. Have you ever planted a seed and then nurtured it into a flower?"

"No, and I really don't care to," I said with honesty. However, I suppose that my tone of voice made me sound rather snotty.

"This is the family room," he said as we walked out of the basement and up a few stairs. There was a large sectional brown leather sofa that looked huge enough to seat at least seven or eight people. At both ends of the sectional there were recliner seats. The oversize sofa even had cup holders and a compartment to keep ice cold. Another large flat-screen television was mounted on the wall along with a complete home theater system. He waited for a response from me, but I only nodded my head. From there we moved into the kitchen, which looked like it was out of a magazine. The refrigerator had a crushed icemaker, there was a center island where food could be prepared, and there was an abundance of cabinet and shelf space. From there it was on to the formal dining room. There was a beautiful wooden table large enough to seat eight people. The table was completely set but looked more like a display rather than a place to eat.

"Follow me and I'll show you to your room," he said as he opened yet another door, which I thought was a closet but it was actually a staircase that led to the upper level of the house.

"Damn, this is a big-ass house," I blurted out my thoughts.

"I'd prefer that you not use foul language. It's not becoming of a lady," Jordan said, and I looked at him like he'd just lost his mind. *I know that he didn't call himself putting me in check*, I thought to myself. *The last thing he has the right to do is discipline me.*

"Whatever," I said as I walked up the stairs. In my mind I didn't see myself staying in this house for very long. I felt like I was intruding on his space anyway. When I reached the top landing there were three bedrooms and a bathroom up there. Grandmother Katie was coming out of the bathroom as we were about to turn and walk down the corridor toward the bedrooms.

"Well, I see you two have finally made it up here," she said with a smile.

"I'm about to show Keysha to her room," Jordan said. I followed him down to the last door, which was closed.

"I think you should open it," he said as he stepped aside. I placed my hand on the handle of the white door, gave it a twist and opened it up. I was completely taken aback by the size of the room. It was huge. There was a beautiful vanity dresser filled with all types of cosmetic products. There was a queen-size canopy bed with linen that matched the curtains, a desk and chair were near the window, as well as a stand that had a small television with a VCR and DVD player built into it.

"I hope you like the room," Jordan said.

"Of course she likes it," answered Grandmother Katie. To tell the truth I felt like I was more like an outsider than I'd ever felt before. It all seemed so fake to me, and I feared that at any moment someone would come and tell me that there was a big mistake and I wouldn't be able to stay. So, in my mind, there was no sense in getting too comfortable, because I knew that dreams didn't come true, and at some point either I'd run away or get mixed up in some juvenile-delinquent mess just like I was expected to.

"Um, can I be alone for a moment?" I asked, turning to face Grandmother Katie and Jordan. Both of them had goofy smiles plastered on their faces. At that moment I felt as if I was the charity case of the century, and I didn't like that feeling.

"Sure, you can have some privacy, honey," said Grandmother Katie.

"Your brother will be home in awhile," said Jordan. That was another thing that was peculiar to me. Jordan spoke so clearly and flawlessly. He didn't sound anything like the men who hung around the empty lot near my old apartment building. He actually spoke like Carlton Banks from the program *The Fresh Prince of Bel-Air.* "Barbara will be home later. We're all going out for a nice family dinner tonight," he announced, and I cringed at the thought of sitting at a dinner table with them.

"I don't have anything to wear," I quickly said, confident that my excuse would get me out of having to go with them.

"Look in the closet over there, honey. Some nice clothes have been purchased for you," said Grandmother Katie, who still had a smile plastered on her face. I just knew that whatever they had purchased for me was all wrong. *Old people have no sense of style,* I thought to myself.

"If you need anything, we'll be down in the family room," Jordan said before he and his mother walked out of the room and shut the door behind them.

chapter 13

I just stood in the center of my bedroom for the longest time, afraid to touch anything. Once I found the courage to move within the space, I went over to the vanity and looked at the products there. It was filled with Proactive Solution skin-care products, cotton balls, Q-tips and an assortment of nail polishes and other makeup items. I opened the top left drawer and discovered it contained feminine hygiene essentials, which I had to admit I was in desperate need of. I went over and sat down at the desk in the room and stared out the window. My view was of the backyard. There was a large tree directly outside of my window that blocked part of my view of the garage and swimming pool. I don't know how long I'd been sitting there but I was startled out of my trance by a knock at the door. I didn't say anything, so the person knocked again. This time a little louder. I got up, moved to the door and opened it.

"What's up, son?" A young boy was at my door. He had caramel skin, a thin trace of hair on his upper lip and an athletic build.

"You're Mike, right?" I asked, trying not to laugh as I studied his appearance more closely. He had a white scarf wrapped around his head, which I assumed was more for fashion than it was for hairstyle. He had a Band-Aid positioned under his left eye, which made him look like a Nelly wannabe. He contorted his face and puckered his lips into an expression he considered to be thuggish, but it only made him look as if he were sitting on the throne with a bad case of constipation. He had on an oversize Akademiks T-shirt with matching Akademiks Armor jeans and a pair of Akademiks gym shoes.

"What? You see something funny?" he asked as he crossed his arms across his chest and tucked his fingers in his armpits. He appeared to be attempting to flex his chest and arm muscles, but he didn't have enough muscle to flex.

"Boy, you are not hard, so don't even try to act like you are some thug with a reputation and a criminal record."

"You don't know me. You don't know the things I've done. I'm a straight gangster. You're in my world now."

"Well, you're the first thirteen-year-old hardened gangster I've seen," I said, thinking he was joking.

"I'm going to be fourteen in a minute," he said, making a gesture with his fingers. It was then that I realized he was serious about the charade he was putting on.

"Whatever, fool," I said and was about to slam the door in his face.

"Girl, why are you hating on me? Is it because I'm so iced-out? Is it because of my grillz?" He smiled at me, and I peeked at his teeth.

"That is not a grillz in your mouth, those are braces," I said. "Who do you think you're trying to fool? Your money is not long, and you are certainly not a baller." I'd suddenly become annoyed with him. I studied him closely for another moment and could tell he was up to no good by the way he shifted his eyes from left to right.

"Okay." He lowered his voice to a loud whisper. "I may not be a baller or a thug but listen up, because I'm only going to say this once. If you want to get along up in here, all you need to do is stay out of my way, mind your own business and don't be up in here trying to act like daddy's little girl. Do you understand what I'm saying, son?" He stepped closer to me as if he wanted to knuckle-up and fight. I wasn't afraid of his scrawny behind at all. I made a sudden move as if I were about to hit him and he flinched with fear.

"Yeah, just what I thought. You're just a little spoiled-ass punk!" I said with a vicious tone in my voice.

"Well at least I don't have a face that looks like pimple paradise. I mean, damn girl, did every zit in the nation take up space on your forehead?" Before I could stop myself, I swung at him. Mike saw the punch coming and quickly moved out of my reach.

"Hey, you don't want to throw down with me. I may not look like it, but I know how to fight," he said as he backed away. I could tell that I'd scared him because his voice trembled.

"You see that I'm not scared, don't you?" I snarled at him, feeling a deep hate for him growing each second that ticked by. "Here is a word of advice for you, Chicken Little," I called him out of his name. "You have to bring some ass in order to kick some ass. If you come at me sideways again, I will beat you down like a crackhead who stole my last two dollars." I gave him the meanest, most threatening glare that my face could form. He didn't say anything, only continued to back away. He went back to his room and shut his door. I went back inside my room and shut the door, as well. I didn't feel good about being in this house at all, but until I could find a place to run away to, this would have to do.

I decided to just chill in the room and pass the time by watching television. I was watching a movie called *Save the Last Dance* starring Julia Stiles. It was about this rich girl who lost her mother and then had to go live in the hood with her father. I suppose I identified with the movie because my situation was reversed. I had to move from the hood with my mother and live like some stuck-up girl in the rich suburbs. The movie was excellent, and I enjoyed watching all the dance moves she and the other characters did in the movie. The movie was just about to reach its climax when I heard Jordan's voice.

"Keysha." I didn't answer him because I was trying to figure why it sounded as if he was in the room with me.

"There is an intercom on the wall next to your closet door. Go over to it and press the 'talk' button to answer me." I looked over at my closet door and noticed the intercom. I did as he instructed.

"We're going to be going to dinner in about a half hour, so start getting ready. We're going to the Outback Steakhouse so jeans will be the appropriate attire to wear."

Appropriate attire, I thought to myself. *He sounds all nerdy.*

"Okay," I answered him back and then sat back on the bed to continue watching my movie. I was dreading looking in the closet at the clothes my grandmother had picked out because I knew they'd be a throwback to the sixties or seventies. After the movie ended I opened the large walk-in closet and flipped the light switch.

"Damn," I spoke aloud. "This closet is big enough to put a bed in." There were two dressers inside the closet along with plenty of shelf space for shoes and other accessories. There was also a large dressing mirror inside. The other thing that freaked me out was each drawer had a small label on it indicating what item of clothing was on the inside. I opened the drawer that said "jeans." To my surprise, Grandmother Katie had pretty good taste. Inside were several pairs of Baby Phat blue jeans.

"This is all right," I said to myself as I opened up other drawers and located tops, underwear and other items. This entire change in my life was like magic. It was like living in a fairy tale, and it just seemed too good to be true. I matched up an outfit that was acceptable to me. I then went into the bathroom and got ready. About fifteen minutes later, I stood in front of my mirror fully dressed fussing with my hair because I was trying to make myself perfect, but my hair wasn't cooperating. Months of neglect and bad styling decisions couldn't be erased in a matter of seconds. I decided to put on my night hair scarf to cover it up just like Toya was so fond of doing. It would just have to do for now until I could get something done with it. I had butterflies in my stomach because I was about to go down and really meet Barbara, my step-mother, who made me feel very uncomfortable. I decided if she was going to be mean to me, then I'd be just as mean to her. I finally got my nerves in order and walked downstairs and into the family room where everyone was sitting and waiting on me.

"It took you long enough, I started growing a gray hair waiting on you," Mike said sarcastically.

Grandmother Katie smacked him on the back of his head. "Watch your manners, Mike." I looked around at each of them and felt as if they were all judging me.

"Why does she have that head rag on, Jordan?"

Barbara tried to whisper in my father's ear, but I heard her. She acted as if I wasn't there and couldn't hear her. I felt as if I wasn't good enough for them. I felt as if I just didn't measure up.

"Just forget it. Y'all go out by yourselves. That's what you want anyway," I said as I rushed back up to my room. I shut the door and began to pace the floor again. I tried to focus my thinking and determine what to do next. The only thing that came to mind was to pack my things, steal any money lying around and take my chances out on the streets.

"Baby, come on and go with us. She didn't mean anything by what she said." Grandmother Katie had just opened my door.

"She doesn't like me," I said. "It was written all over her face."

"Give it time, Keysha. Your existence is news to all of us. We all have to make some adjustments and make room in our lives for you." I plopped down on the edge of the bed and placed my face in my hands.

"Keysha, I really want you to have dinner with us," said Jordan, who was now in my bedroom, too. I looked up at him and saw a part of me in his eyes. For a brief moment I felt some sense of a connection and wanted to hug him but I didn't. I just felt angry with everything and everyone.

"Can I sit down next to you?" he asked.

"It's your house," I answered.

"When I look at you, I see myself," he said. "I see a part of me that I feel like I should know but I don't, and that hurts. Perhaps I'm moving too fast, but I want to give you all of the things that you've never had. I want to make up for that. I can give you a decent place to live, nice clothes and some sense of stability. What I can't give you is the time we've lost. There is so much to learn and understand, but we have to give things time."

"He's right, you know," said Grandmother Katie. "There are so many things about me and our family that you need to know, learn and understand. I want you to have that sense of belonging, but I know it's not going to happen overnight. A sense of belonging comes from within, and when you get that feeling hold on to it, because it also means that you're beginning to feel loved." It's just downright frightening how Grandmother Katie could read me.

"Let me see your hair." Grandmother Katie walked over to me, and I allowed her to remove my scarf.

"It's not so bad, honey. We just have to let it grow out a little and take care of it better," she said as she took a closer look at my hair. "We can just brush it back and you'll be fine." Grandmother Katie picked up the brush that was sitting atop the vanity. She sat down at the foot of my bed and asked me to sit on the floor between her thighs.

"I want you to know that I'm always here for you,

Keysha. I want you to be able to come to me and confide in me. I want you to know about my history just as much as I want to know about yours. I don't even know what your favorite color or food is. Just like you've missed out, so has this family," Grandmother Katie explained as she continued working with my hair.

"She hates me, doesn't she?" I asked, referring to Barbara.

"No, she doesn't hate you at all. She just has to adjust to this change in her life," said Grandmother Katie as she brushed the other side of my hair. Her brush strokes were soft and comforting.

"There is a lot that you have to understand. One of which is that we've always wanted two children, a boy and a girl. We were able to have a son together but medical complications have prevented us from having additional children," said Jordan.

"Life is like that sometimes," Grandmother Katie continued. "You can plan out the perfect life for yourself, but if your plans don't match God's plan, then I'm afraid that you're setting yourself up to deal with a lot of heartache."

"I wonder what God has planned for my mother?" I spoke aloud as I thought about what Grandmother Katie said. No one could give me an answer to my question. The room was silent for a moment, and then Barbara walked in.

"Listen, why don't we just order pizza tonight," she

said, refusing to make eye contact with me. "I'm not feeling too good, and I just want to lie down."

"Are you okay?" Jordan asked as he draped his arm around her shoulder.

"I'm just not feeling good. Come help me lie down," she said, and Jordan escorted her to her room. At that moment I felt jealousy raise its ugly head. I mean, for the first time I was actually starting to feel some sort of connection to my father, and she came up and took him away from me. She'd had him for years and I couldn't get twenty minutes alone with him without her interrupting us. I hated her for intruding on my time with him. It wasn't fair.

chapter 14

The following morning, I woke up and for the first time in ages I felt very well rested. The bed I was sleeping in was the most comfortable bed I'd ever been on. It was just right; the linen smelled fresh, and the pillows were soft and fluffy. Just as I was enjoying my blissful moment, I was startled out of my mind by the presence of Barbara sitting in the vanity chair staring at me. It freaked me out because I didn't know what to think or what was about to go down.

"What's going on?" I asked as I quickly sat upright in my bed.

"Did you sleep well?" she asked with a wicked undertone in her voice and an evil glint in her eyes.

"I slept fine. Why are you in my room?" I didn't like the invasion of my privacy one bit.

"This is my house. I can go into any room of my choice." I couldn't argue that point with her so I didn't.

"You and I need to have a little girl-to-girl chat," Barbara said as she leaned forward in the seat and locked her gaze on me.

"You're Jordan's daughter, there is no denying that. You look more like him than Mike does. And since you were obviously conceived before Jordan and I were married, I can't hold your existence against him. Especially since he didn't know about you. But that's not what I'm here to talk about."

"Well, get to the point," I snapped at her. I didn't like her attitude or the way she was talking to me and I wanted to let her know it. It was bad enough that I didn't measure up to her standards but now she was about to reinforce my shortcomings.

"Yeah, we need to get some things ironed out. According to your social worker, Maggie, you're sexually active." I twisted my lips and rolled my eyes at her.

"Yeah, I know about it." She paused briefly. "There are some rules and boundaries we need to get ironed out. You will not set one foot back in this house if you go out and get yourself knocked up. I don't care if you are Jordan's daughter, getting pregnant out of wedlock is not acceptable."

"Jordan knocked up my mama out of wedlock," I reminded her.

"That was then, but this is now. I expect you to do well in school. Failing grades will not be tolerated and will be dealt with accordingly."

"You know what, I'm not even trying to hear you. You don't know anything about me and you're not trying to, either. So you can just talk to my hand." I held my hand up in front of her face.

"Do you know why I feel this way, little girl?" I didn't answer her question.

"Because I think you're going to follow in your mother's and your grandmother's footsteps and become a jailbird and a failure."

"Whatever," I snarled at her. "I'm not even trying to go to jail," I said to her, even though I felt as if some situation would befall me and I'd end up in juvenile court for one reason or another.

"Then prove me wrong," she said. "Prove me wrong by shocking the daylights out of me."

I looked up at the ceiling because I didn't want to listen to her anymore.

"No boys are allowed in the house without an adult present."

"So does that mean that Mike can't come in when I'm here all alone?" I was being a smart-ass because I didn't like her rules at all.

"You know what I mean. I don't want any of your male friends from your old neighborhood visiting this house," she said, raising her voice at me. I could tell that my indifference and lack of fear were irritating her. I was getting a twisted joy out of it.

"So what are you trying to say? You think that just

because I'm from the inner city that all of my friends are thugs, prostitutes and dope dealers?"

"Let's just say I wouldn't be surprised if they were." She moved my hand from in front of her face.

"I guess you don't know or see that Mike wants to be a thug. His pants were sagging more than anyone I've ever known."

"He's just going through a phase, that's all. As long as he continues to be an honor student, I can live with his temporary fascination with hip-hop culture."

"You have an answer for everything, don't you?"

"You know, Grandmother Katie will be going home soon." She stood up. "And when she does, it will just be the two of us. And you should know I'm the only queen in this house."

"Is that all?" I asked, glad to see she was about to leave. It was now very clear to me that we would never get along.

"For now. I'm sure we'll have future conversations, because I know you're going to mess up." After that comment, she walked over to the door but stopped just before exiting.

"Oh, by the way, Grandmother Katie is taking you to my hairstylist so that your hair can be taken care of. I can't have you walking around looking bad about the head because it makes me look bad." When she turned her back again, I stuck my tongue out at her in a gesture of defiance.

* * *

I really liked my Grandmother Katie. She had a way of knowing just what to say and how to say it without being offensive or mean-spirited. I also liked her because she didn't judge me. She accepted me for who I was and saw me as a young lady who was very badly bruised. I fell in love with her for understanding me in ways that I didn't understand myself. I enjoyed talking to her more than I did Jordan, my snotty brother, Mike, and my wicked stepmother, Barbara. What made her even more special was that we'd read some of the same books and had fun talking about them. Grandmother Katie said that once she returned home she'd ship me a few books that she thought would interest me. She was planning to leave on Wednesday, which I was rather sad about because she was the only person I felt comfortable talking to.

Late Sunday evening, I was sitting in my room with my back resting against the headboard of my bed. I was feeling rather sad because I had gone to the hairstylist and she'd had to cut most of my hair off because it was too damaged. I was also missing my mom and wished she and I could do things like going to get our hair and nails done. Grandmother Katie knocked on my door and asked if she could come in.

"How are you feeling this evening?" she asked. That was another thing that I liked about her. She seemed to be genuinely concerned about me.

"Kind of sad," I said.

"Do you want to talk about it?" she asked. I moved my feet so that she could sit on the bed with me.

"All my hair is gone, and I just miss my mother a little," I admitted.

"Well, darling, your hair is nice. I bet in time you will grow to like it. And if I were you, I think I would miss my mother, too. You should take some time and go see about her."

"I'm not ready. I mean, the last time I saw her she was mean to me, and I just don't feel like getting my feelings hurt again."

"It wasn't easy for you growing up, was it?" she asked.

"I guess not. I mean, I never thought that we had it bad or anything like that. Things were just the way they were. I thought it was normal."

"Tell me something about you that you really like about yourself."

"What do you mean?" I asked because I was confused by the question.

"Tell me something about you as a person that you really like about yourself."

"Nothing. My hair is whacked out, my skin looks like volcanoes are about to erupt on it, my butt is like my mother's, it's too big for my body and guys are always making me feel self-conscious about it."

"Those are all of the things on the outside. Tell me what you like about you, the person?" she asked.

"No one has ever asked me that question before." I paused in thought. "I don't know what I like about me. I feel like I'm just here."

"Well, I've only known you for a short time and let me tell you what I see. You're a very smart and shapely young woman who has been able to survive on her own with very little adult supervision. That's a sign of character. You have a strong mind that guides you and hungers to learn, and to me that's a sign of a very intelligent young woman. Keysha, I want you to work on the mental voices in your head that feed you negative information about yourself. You don't need to be your own worst enemy. When you hear the voices of doubt and self-defeat, you have to quiet them with more positive things about who you are and what you can do and accomplish. If you belittle yourself, you only open the door for others to do the same."

"Wow, how are you able to do that?" I asked.

"Do what?" she asked. I began trying to express myself with my hands as I spoke.

"You have a way of getting around me and my barriers. You know how to go directly to my fears without me telling you. What are you, gifted or something?" Grandmother Katie smiled at me.

"I listen with my heart and soul," she said, which confused me even more.

"No one has ever called me intelligent before," I

admitted, holding my head down. "Everyone has always expected me to mess up. When my mother and other grandmother thought I was pregnant, they were happy because it meant more money would be coming into the house." I swallowed hard because I was embarrassed by that fact. "I love my Grandmother Rubylee, but all she ever does is try to steal from people. I don't want to be like her or my mother. I don't want to rip people off, but that's all people expect me to do. Even Barbara doesn't think much of me."

"Listen, baby. Let me tell you something. You don't have to be like your mother and grandmother at all. The choices you make are your own, and if you choose *not* to follow in their footsteps then you will not. You are in control of what you do, not them, not me and certainly not Barbara."

"Tell me honestly, why doesn't Barbara like me?"

"Barbara cares more than you think. She just has a different way of expressing it. She may be rather blunt and frank, but she means well. You wouldn't have made it into this house if she had not agreed to it. Give her credit for that. She may be stern—"

"And stuck-up," I interrupted her. She smiled and nodded her head.

"She has her moments. I think that once you and Barbara get past this odd time you'll discover that you guys aren't as different as you might think you are," she said, being sure she'd selected the right words.

"What about my daddy? What was he like growing up?" I asked.

"Oh, your father was a mischievous and a curious young man," she said, chuckling as she thought about Jordan as a young man. "When he was around eight or nine, he'd heard from somewhere that you could dig your way to China. So he went into the garage and got a shovel and dug up all of my flowers because he wanted to see if he could dig to China." I laughed at the silliness of my father's logic. "I made him replant every flower he dug up. As quiet as it's kept, that's probably why he likes gardening so much. Your father is a very loving and generous man, but he also likes control and can be stern and hard. However, if you're ever in a jam, he'll never leave your side."

I didn't really believe everything she said, but I took it for what it was worth. "What about Mike? What's your take on him?" I asked.

"He's just a typical teenaged boy trying to find out who he is. He's at a very impressionable age."

"So the thug thing is just an act?" I asked, looking for confirmation.

"Mike is just imitating what he sees rappers do on the television. He's lived a privileged lifestyle, and as far as I know, has never been near a bad neighborhood. His mother sees to that." I was quiet for the moment because once again I was feeling jealous. I just couldn't understand why he ended up with everything and I ended up with nothing.

"Listen, I'm going to leave my phone number with you. I want you to call me if you ever need anything or just need someone to talk to."

"Okay," I said.

"Keysha, can you do me a favor?"

"What?" I asked.

"Smile for me. You don't smile much and you have such a beautiful and warm smile."

"I really haven't had much to smile about. Smiling would mean that I'm happy and that everything is going okay, but it's not."

"It's not going right, even just a little bit?" she asked.

"Well, yeah, on the surface all of this appears to be perfect, but at times I wonder if it's too good to be true and what did I do to deserve this?"

"You see, that's the negative voice you need to work on. You shouldn't say what I did to deserve this. You should say 'I do deserve to live where I feel safe and loved.'"

"Okay, I'll work on that," I said.

chapter 15

Jordan and Maggie took care of the details regarding getting my records transferred to Thornwood High School, which was my new school. Going to a new school as a new kid is never easy. In my case, going to two new schools in such a short time was even more difficult. I didn't know anyone—well, I knew Mike, but he was a jackass. I didn't know exactly where my classes were, and I didn't know which teachers would be mean and difficult, so on my first day I was very nervous. I was worried about the way I looked and how people would perceive me. I was worried about my new haircut because I knew girls talked about other girls with short hair. I was paranoid that someone would say something mean about my pimples, which actually were looking a lot better since Grandmother Katie had shown me how to use Proactive Solution. But still I had some concerns about self-image.

Thornwood High was within walking distance of

the house. I thought for sure Mike would at least walk with me, but he had football practice at 6:00 a.m. on my first day. As I approached the school, I saw kids hanging out in the school parking lot. Kids were pulling up in Mustangs and BMWs, which was unheard of at my other schools. I looked over at a group of girls who were standing next to a silver Mercedes. I listened as they sang the lyrics to a Missy Elliott Song.

"Why don't you just take a picture, it lasts longer," said one girl who noticed me studying them. It was clear that I'd annoyed her. I walked away quickly before I ended up getting into an altercation on my first day. I walked through a set of large brown doors and searched for a sign that would point me in the direction of my guidance counselor's office. I had to stop and meet my guidance counselor, some dude named Mr. Sanders, to pick up my class schedule. I didn't see any signs so I asked a guy who was passing by.

"Excuse me, can you tell me where the guidance counselor's office is?"

"Go all the way down the hall and make a left," he said and continued on his way. I followed his directions and a short time later entered the guidance counselor's office.

"Excuse me," I said to the receptionist. "I'm here to see Mr. Sanders."

"Do you have an appointment?" she asked.

"Yes, I'm a new student. He's expecting me."

"Name," she said without looking at me.

"Keysha Wiley, I mean, it's Keysha Kendall now."

"Oh, yes. We've heard about you." I quickly caught an attitude.

"What have you heard?" I asked. She didn't answer, only looked at me as if I'd offended her.

"Are you Keysha?" A very tall Caucasian man with a round belly and thick glasses appeared from one of the offices.

"Yes," I answered.

"Well, come on in," he said with a pleasant voice. I entered his office and sat down. He shut the door and took a seat behind his desk, which was very junky. There were papers piled up everywhere.

"You'll have to excuse my desk. My student assistant is out with the flu," he said as he searched through the mountain of papers and folders on his desk.

"Here we go," he said once he found my file. He leaned back in his chair and studied it for a moment before speaking.

"The scores that have come in from your other schools aren't very impressive, that is with the exception of your literature grade. You did well in that subject." I wanted to explain the reason I did so poorly was because my mother never prepared me for school and how I was expected to become pregnant and bring a welfare check into the house, but I didn't think he would care to hear my drama.

"We're going to monitor your progress and see how

well you perform academically. This is a tough school, Keysha, and the teachers here expect nothing but the best." He glanced up at me. I didn't know what to say. School for me was just a place I could go to get away from my mother. I hadn't paid attention to my grades since middle school. After I saw that my mother couldn't care less, I stopped putting forth an effort. Mr. Sanders exhaled loudly.

"Here is your schedule." He handed me a sheet of paper and began to explain it to me.

"Your math scores are very low so we've placed you in a remedial class." I cringed when I heard that. "Now this doesn't mean you have to stay there. If you can prove yourself, we'll move up to a basic math class, and if you do well there, you can move on to a class that's at the correct level. Math is the first class that you have. Second period you're in a basic science class because your other school didn't offer a science program. Third period you have gym, fourth period you have study hall, then lunch, social studies and finally literature. Is that okay?"

"Do I have a choice?" I asked.

"No, you don't," he answered me honestly. "But I'll tell you the same thing I tell all of my other students. School is what you make of it. If you don't put forth an effort, you're going to get poor results. You're responsible for the decisions you make regarding your education."

"I understand," I said.

"Come on, I'll show you where your locker is and then walk you to your first class so that you don't get a tardy slip."

When I walked into my math class, everyone stopped what they were doing and looked at me. Mr. Sanders spoke with the teacher briefly, and then I was instructed to sit next to this chick who was wearing all black. I mean, she was the strangest-looking white girl that I'd ever seen. Her hair was raven black, her eye shadow was black, her lipstick was black and her fingernail polish was black. She had multiple piercings in both ears, her bottom lip was pierced and all of her earrings were black. The girl looked like the daughter of Morticia from *The Addams Family*, but she was nowhere near as sexy or as cool as the character Morticia. I cautiously sat next to her because I didn't know if she was diseased or something. Shortly after Mr. Sanders left, the teacher gave me a math book and opened it up to the section we were going over. She told me to follow along, so I took out my math notebook and a pencil. The class was studying basic addition and subtraction.

"Hey, girl," whispered the chick wearing all black. I nervously glanced over at her. She stuck out her tongue and flicked it back and forth against her lips, making an odd noise. Her tongue was pierced, as well. *This chick is crazy as hell,* I thought to myself.

I looked at her clothing more closely. She had on a black top, with black jeans and black combat boots. At that moment, I told myself that my problems weren't so bad.

"This class totally sucks," she whispered but I didn't respond. "I know you can hear me," she said but I continued to ignore her.

"Ahhh, you're a new chick," she said. "I'm going to have to break you in, girl." I was horrified at the thought of exactly what she meant by that.

The bell rang and I pulled out my course schedule to see what room my science class was in.

"Let me see your schedule," asked the girl. I hesitated.

"Come on, let me see the damn thing. I'm not going to eat it." I was still hesitant.

"Look, you're new, right?"

"Yes," I said.

"That means you don't have a frigging clue as to where you're going. Let me see your schedule and I'll tell you which way to go." I handed it over to her. She began to bob her head up and down.

"Oh, cool. We have the next four classes together."

"You're kidding, right?" I asked.

"Nope. Looks like that jackass Mr. Sanders thought you were going to be a problem child so he stuck you in all of the classes with problem kids."

"How do you know that?" I asked.

"Because only the problem kids get low test scores

and end up in a classroom full of rejects. Like you and me." I looked at her like she was crazy.

"I'm Liz." She stuck out her hand for me to shake it. It was the first time I'd noticed that all of her fingers had black rings on them.

"I'm Keysha," I said as I shook her hand.

"Come on, stick with me. I'll make sure you get to your classes." We walked out of the room and into an overcrowded hallway filled with students. As we made our way through the crowd I heard other students boldly degrading Liz.

"Aaaaaa—It's God-Lizard," said some basketball jock.

"Aaaaa—It's Hillbilly Bob from Hillbilly Heaven," Liz quickly fired back.

"It's the Lizard Wizard," said another student.

"Ooh, it's Loser Lou," Liz said as she gave him the middle finger.

It was strange watching how Liz maneuvered through that crowded hallway and through all of the teasing and wisecracks. I felt bad for her and began to think that she was misunderstood, just like me.

We entered the science room and I followed her to the back table and sat next to her on one of the stools. We were the first students in the class.

"Look, I need a lab partner, so what do you say? You and I can be partners." I was hesitant at first because I wasn't sure that I even wanted to be around her.

"Look, you're new. No one is going to pick you and since I don't have a partner, the brilliant science teacher is going to pair us up anyway. So let's just cut the middleman and be partners."

"What's up, Lazy Liz?" said some guy who had just walked in.

"Bite me! Groovy Grover," Liz shot back.

"Groovy Grover?" I laughed out loud.

"Yeah, that's Garret Groover. He's a complete idiot. Don't pay him any attention."

"Girl, I'm not trying to get any of your fleas," said Grover. Liz gave him the middle finger and stuck her tongue out at him.

"Look, just sit someplace else. If you don't want to be my partner then I don't care. Just go and sit someplace else and leave me alone," said Liz.

"No," I said. "I'll be your partner." I felt sorry for her.

"Cool, we can both flunk the class together." She laughed and so did I.

chapter 16

So where are you from?" asked Liz. We were now on the way to lunch together. There was nothing feminine about Liz. She walked like a man and talked like a man and had a very strong presence about her. Regardless of the nasty comments a few students made about her, Liz couldn't have cared less, and I suppose I was drawn to her because of her strength. She was strong in ways that I didn't think I was.

"Chicago," I said.

"Really? What side of the city?"

"South side," I answered her.

"Cool. I used to live on the north side a few years back. Up in the Ravenswood area. I still have a lot of friends in that part of town. They're much cooler than these stuck-up rich kids out here." We turned left down another corridor and I could see the cafeteria ahead of us. "So how did you end up at this school?"

"It's a long story," I said.

"Hey, I've got nothing but time," Liz said as she held the cafeteria door open for me. The place was noisy and packed with kids.

"Come on, the line is over here." I followed Liz and stood in line.

"The pizza sucks. Never eat it because I think they spit on it. The fries and burgers are good but never, under any circumstances, eat the fish sticks. If you do, you'll spend the afternoon with a bad case of the runs."

"Eeew," I said.

"Exactly," Liz responded. "The people in this school are so lame. The cheerleaders are way too damn catty. The jocks, or the jockstraps as I call them, are completely into their bodies. They're all brawn and no brains, if you know what I mean."

"Yeah, my brother is like that," I said, thinking about the incident I had with Mike yesterday.

"You have a brother who goes here?" Liz asked.

"Yeah, his name is Mike Kendall."

"You're kidding me?" Liz asked completely surprised.

"No. Why did you respond like that?"

"The kid is only a freshman, and he is one of the most popular kids on campus. He came into the school and broke the sprint record for the fifty-yard dash. The old record was 5.5 seconds and he ran it in 5.3 seconds. The football and track coaches were on him like flies on shit. I heard that he's the only freshman on the varsity football squad."

"I don't know much about all of that," I admitted.

"Well, just FYI for you. He thinks everyone likes him, but it's only because of his speed and the fact that your dad works for the hottest radio station in town. People have been blowing his head up because they're hoping to get some free concert tickets or something."

"Does he know kids are just using him?" I asked.

"I don't know. Maybe he does and maybe he doesn't. Either way, the guy is popular. It's practically unheard of to be a freshman and playing football on the varsity squad."

Once we got our food, I followed Liz around the cafeteria to a table filled with other students who were dressed like Liz. Everyone had piercings, spiked and multicolored hair, and damn near all of them wore black.

"Yo, listen up." Liz got everyone's attention.

"This is Keysha, she's new and is going to be hanging out with us." I said hello to everyone and they just nodded.

"So what's your story?" Liz asked as she dipped a few of her French fries in a small cup of ketchup.

"My story is real jacked-up."

"Hell, honey, I've already figured that one out. Give me details." Liz leaned forward so that she could hear me clearly.

"My grandmother was arrested for bank robbery and is serving time in prison. My mother is also serving time. When she got arrested, I had to live in a group home for a while."

"Oh, man, you too? I knew that I liked you the moment I saw you. Which whacked out facility were you at?"

"I was at a place on the south side. You were in a group home too?" I asked.

"Hell, worse. I was at Sunnyville."

"Sunnyville?" I asked, confused.

"You know, the nuthouse. They wanted to evaluate my mind for a while," she said, bugging her eyes wide open as if her mind was some great mysterious phenomenon. I was intrigued by her story and wanted to know more.

"My dad was my world. I was his princess." I read Liz's expression and I could tell that what she was about to tell me was deeply personal. "He and my mom got divorced a few years back. I can't stand my mom because she's such a bitch, so I asked to go live with my dad. He was the coolest dad a girl could have. He was a soldier in the army. When the whole Iraq War thing broke out he was called to duty. To make a long story short, his unit was escorting a supply truck and they were ambushed. He was killed."

"I'm so sorry to hear that," I said, feeling really bad. I knew that it had to have been hard to know her father all of her life and then lose him.

"Anyway, when I got the news I didn't take it very well," she said, and then she just stopped talking. I waited for her to continue but she didn't. It was as if she'd locked up her feelings about it or something.

"So that's why you wear all black, because you're in mourning, right?" I asked. She suddenly slapped the palms of her hands down on the table, making a loud sound that startled me.

"See." She pointed her finger at me. "Why is it that you can see that but my all-knowing mother thought I'd flipped out and shipped me off to the damn nuthouse where a weirdo tried to fry my damn brain?" Liz was very passionate as well as angry.

"So, you're back at home with your mother?" I asked.

"Yeah, and her new boyfriend, who has moved in with us. I don't like him at all. He keeps telling my mother that I'm headed for trouble and blah, blah, blah." I didn't ask Liz any more questions because she appeared to be on the edge and I didn't want to push her. *Hell, and I thought I had it bad,* I thought to myself.

I met Liz after school, and since her house was in the same direction as mine, we walked home together. I wanted to know more about her dad so I asked another question.

"So, what was your dad like?"

"He was cool. If I said, 'Hey, dad, can I get fifty bucks to go shopping with,' he'd give me sixty and say get something to eat, as well." Liz continued, "He was always around whenever I needed him. If my bike was on a flat, he'd fix it for me. When I wanted to learn how to swim, he'd spend his Saturday mornings teaching me how. When I was selling Girl Scout cookies, he made sure that my order sheet was always filled. I loved him. I could always depend on him for anything. He was the type of dad who always bought me something when we went shopping. Even if it was the dumbest toy ever made. He'd buy it for me because I wanted it."

"What do you miss the most about him?" I asked.

"His smile, his laugh and his scent." Liz paused in thought. "I suppose the thing I miss the most is him coming into my room at night and tucking me in. I know it sounds corny, but I'd lie in the bed and he'd wrap me up like a mummy and then hug me. That was the best feeling in the world." I saw Liz wipe a tear away from her eyes. I felt her pain so I hugged her.

"Ew, you're hugging Lesbo Liz," said a group of guys who were walking past us. I didn't care what the other kids thought. I just felt she could use a hug, and she accepted it.

"I hate this damn war," Liz said as she backed away from me. "I'm sorry for dumping on you like this."

"It's okay," I said. "I can understand how you must feel." We walked a little farther and finally reached my house.

"Nice house," Liz said. "It's big."

"Maybe you could come over sometime. We could sit around and listen to music or something."

Liz laughed. "Or we could get online and hang out in a chat room and see what kind of perverts are out there."

"I'm not too sure about that one," I said, laughing.

"Well, don't knock it until you try it. It's kind of fun and exciting to talk with someone who is in another part of the country or the world."

"Well, I'd better go. I'll see you tomorrow," I said. Liz said goodbye and continued on her way. I walked down my driveway toward the house feeling good that I'd met a nice person, even though she was kind of odd.

chapter 17

Once I got closer to the house, I saw my father in the greenhouse planting flowers in a clay pot. He saw me and waved and I waved back. Since he was alone, I thought it would be a good time to go and talk to him. I walked across the grass and entered the greenhouse through the side door. There was a small black radio with paint spots on it on top of a small furnace that was built into the glass of the greenhouse. A song called "Quiet Storm" by Smokey Robinson was playing on the radio. I remembered the song because Grandmother Rubylee played it often.

"Hey," I said.

"Hey, how was your first day at school?" he asked as he looked over his shoulder at me.

"It was okay. It went better than I thought it would. So why aren't you at work?" I asked.

"I wanted to be here when you got home so I took off early today. I want to make sure things go well and that you get settled in and used to being here. Do you like the school?" he asked as he turned the radio down a little.

"It's okay. It's just a school," I said as I took a seat on a small chair that was near me.

"So what are you planting?" I asked.

"Mums, for the fall season," he said. "Do you want to help me place them in these pots?"

"No," I answered. The last thing I wanted to do was play in the dirt.

"Are you sure? It's very relaxing."

I chuckled because being relaxed about anything was foreign to me. Everything in my life thus far was drama and tension.

"You know, I would imagine you have a lot questions." He stopped playing in the dirt and looked directly at me. "I'll answer any questions you have, Keysha. No matter how trivial or adult they are. You have a right to know, and I'm here for you," he said. I wasn't used to someone speaking to me with a calm and soothing voice. I was accustomed to shouting and yelling to get my point across. He smiled at me, and I felt funny because his smile reminded me so much of my own and it was weird to see it on someone else's face. I was quiet for a long moment as I tried to organize all of the questions in my head.

"Let me start. I want to tell you that as a man, and your father, I'm always in your corner. I'm always on your side, and I have your best interests in mind. I want you to know that about me," he said. I swallowed hard as I thought about the first question I wanted to ask.

"Go ahead," he said. "No question is too tough."

"How did you meet my mother?" I wanted to know. Jordan pulled up another chair and sat down directly in front of me so that we could look at each other.

"I know you may find this hard to believe, but I was the nerd in the family," he said, and I started laughing because he was a nerd to me through and through.

"I was the straight-A student who actually loved school. Unlike some of our family members, I grew up in the suburbs as opposed to the inner city. At family gatherings my other cousins, who were much worldlier than I was at the time, made fun of me. They criticized my intelligence, called me a sellout and teased me about my lack of street sense. My cousin Simon was the ringleader, but for some reason I envied him, because no matter how crazy and cocky he was, he seemed to always be able to get the prettiest girls. By the time I was twenty-one years old, I was a college student with a healthy appetite for a good party. I'd been square all of my life and going away to college helped me out of my shell. I'd only gone to a few parties, because at my core I was an overachiever who couldn't stand getting anything less than a superior grade. Anyway, during spring break that year, your grandfather gave me five hundred dollars for being a straight-A student. Your grandparents loved to brag about that sort of thing, and

Simon heard about the bonus money and convinced me to come and hang out with him. He said that he knew of some great parties where there would be plenty of girls. He assured me that I'd have a great time. Simon was true to his word. He took me to a jumping party. In true Simon fashion, he was able to hook up with some of the prettiest girls there. And in my true fashion, I struck out with every girl I spoke to. Eventually, Simon came up to me and said, 'There is a girl over there who wants to get to know you better.' He pointed her out to me and I thought, Wow, she's a nice-looking girl. 'Don't blow it this time by acting all nerdy,' he said. I walked over to the girl and introduced myself. I was so nervous that when I went to shake her hand I inadvertently knocked her drink out of her hand. I was a complete klutz. After I cleaned up the spill, she told me her name was Justine. I asked her how old she was and she told me that she was eighteen. A few more drinks, a little conversation and several dances later, we were really enjoying each other. One thing led to another, and we had a fling that same evening."

"So, I'm just a lust baby," I said, feeling really bad about myself. I suppose that in some weird way I was hoping that there was at least some type of relationship between him and my mother.

"Keysha, you have to understand that my mind-set at that time was much different than it is now and don't call yourself that. You're a beautiful young lady."

I wanted to say, "yeah, whatever," but I didn't. I just listened.

"The next day I woke up in Simon's spare bedroom with a massive hangover. As I got dressed, I searched my pocket and I noticed that all of my money was gone. I thought perhaps Simon was holding it for me, but as we talked about what happened the prior evening he began laughing at me. He told me, 'Fool, you never take that type of money to a house party in the hood. You let that young girl get you for five hundred big ones.' He blamed me for the loss of my cash. I got angry and demanded that he call Justine so that I could get my money but he refused to do it, stating he couldn't be responsible for getting me cut or beat up. I was so disgusted by everything that I left Simon's apartment and came back home. A few months later at a family holiday gathering I ran into Simon. Myself and a few other male cousins were hanging out in the garage shooting the breeze. Simon let it slip that he and Justine had actually set me up and split the money that your grandfather had given to me. To humiliate me even more, he announced that Justine wasn't eighteen years old, she was much younger than what she led me to believe. It was then that I realized that not only was Simon petty, but he was actually jealous and envious of me. Simon and I fell out after that. I never trusted him again or went to any other parties with him."

"So what happened after that?" I asked.

"I wanted to forget about the entire episode so I left the garage and went back into the house. I went on with my life, Keysha. I summed up the incident with Justine and Simon as one of life's lessons. I just wanted to have a good time. I wasn't thinking about the consequences of my actions. I never knew your mom had gotten pregnant that night. I was never told about it, and I don't know what the circumstances were with your mom at the time that left doubt in her mind as to who your father was. I made a bad judgment call that night. I never thought that my mistake would lead to your birth."

"So I guess I'm the poster child for unprotected sex." I was being both sarcastic and truthful.

"You're not the poster child for anything. Keysha, none of this is your fault."

"What?" I asked, not sure if I'd heard him correctly.

"I said none of this is your fault. What I did was beyond your control. I'm so sorry that I wasn't available to you as a father. I'm so sorry for anything that you've had to go through as a result of my absence." When Jordan said that I felt better.

"Tell me something about you?" I asked. "I barely know you. Like, what's your favorite color, and what is your favorite food?" Jordan smiled at me, and I smiled back at him.

"I'm not sure that I have a favorite color but my

favorite food is macaroni and cheese." Jordan laughed again. His laugh made me laugh.

"I know how to cook. I could make you some if you'd like," I said.

"I'd like it very much if you made me some."

"Okay, I have another question," I said, feeling butterflies dancing in my stomach. At that moment I felt the little girl within me come forward and ask questions that I never could.

"Have your ever sat at the beach and built a sand castle?"

"I used to build them all the time when I was a boy. I learned how to do it from a guy on the beach in Miami, Florida. We used to vacation there every summer. I used to build them and pretend that I was riding up to it on my horse."

"Really?" I asked, filled with excitement.

"Yes," he answered.

"Let me ask you a question," Jordan said. "Are you happy that you know who I am now?" I didn't know how to answer that question. I had to think about it for a minute.

"I guess a part of me is glad that I can put a face and name to my father, but another part of me just isn't very sure about you."

"Okay, I can understand that. I have another question. Tell me something that you really enjoy doing."

I was about to tell him about all of the books I'd read

and how much I loved reading, but Barbara walked up
and interrupted us.

"Jordan," she spoke directly to him without so much
as saying a word to me. "I need to speak with you."

"Give me a minute," Jordan said, wanting to
continue our conversation.

"This can't wait. I need to speak with you right now,
in private." I rolled my eyes at that heifer. She didn't
want or need to speak with him. She just couldn't stand
the fact that I was spending time with my daddy.
Barbara locked her gaze on me for a moment, and I
could tell that she didn't like the fact that Jordan and
I were spending time with each other. I felt as if I was
competing with her and I was ready to fight her. It
wasn't fair in my mind. She'd known him for years and
wasn't willing to give me one hour alone with him. I
began to think of mean things I could do to her. In my
mind I felt there wasn't enough room for the both of
us.

"I need you to help me go over my campaign literature."

"Campaign literature?" I said aloud.

"Yes, I'm running for re-election as president of the
school board. There is no need for your help. It's a little
too complicated for you."

Oh, no, she didn't just say that to me. I was about to
snap the hell out on her, but Jordan didn't let me.

"We'll talk some more later on, okay?" Jordan said,
looking at me. "I promise. I have so much more that I

want to share with you. I need to tell you about the history of our family." I calmed down and agreed that it was okay with me if we spoke later on.

chapter 18

Later that evening, I was sitting in my room at my desk listening to an Alicia Keys song. I loved her voice and her style. I was thinking about my Grandmother Rubylee and decided to write her a letter. I was about to pull out my notepad and begin when there was a knock at my door. I looked over my shoulder and Mike was standing in my doorway holding his football uniform. There were green grass stains all over it.

"What's up, son?" There he goes calling me out of my name again. I swear I was going to beat him down for that, I thought.

"My name isn't son," I reminded him.

"So are you into girls or what?" he boldly asked.

"Excuse you." I contorted my face into an angry expression.

"Yo, I heard that you were, like, all out in the open

hugging up on Lesbo Liz. I just want to know. Are you into girls or what?"

"Go away, Mike," I said, not wanting to answer his dumb question.

"You certainly know how to pick a friend. Liz is a real whack job. She's crazy. I've heard all kinds of crazy stories about her."

"All of the stories you've heard are probably all false," I said as I got up and moved toward him.

"No, I don't think so. That chick isn't working with a full deck, you know what I'm saying?"

"No, I don't know what you're saying." I was now standing in front of him. He looked me up and down as if I repulsed him.

"Well, you two deserve each other. And just so you know, I got people watching you, girl. One false move and I'm going to hear about it." I slammed the door in his face. *Damn jackass*, I thought to myself. I went over to the radio and channel surfed until I found a station that was playing music that reflected the somber mood I was in. I sat back down at my desk and began to write my letter.

Dear Grandma,

I don't know what it's like for you being locked up but my guess is that it's no fun. I miss you. I miss hearing your voice, even though you yelled and shouted a lot. I miss lying in the bed with you and your cooking. I guess I'll never fully understand why and how you ended up where you are, but I wanted you to know that I still love you. I'm not sure if you've heard yet, but Justine is back in jail. She was arrested on some drug-related issue with an old friend of hers. When she got locked up, I ended up having to live in a group home. Being there was no picnic and I was really afraid most of the time. I was afraid of being left all alone like that. I didn't know anyone in the place, and I sort of got to the point where I didn't care what happened to me. A good thing that happened is I found my biological father. How I found him is a long story but I live with him now. He has a big house in the suburbs and I have my own room. Can you believe that? I've never had my own room before. Getting to know him is both easy and hard. I'm really trying hard to let our relationship develop naturally, but at times I get angry and mad that my life wasn't as perfect as it could have been.

I have a stepbrother named Mike. He's a suburban boy who wants to be a thug. Let me tell you, that boy doesn't have an ounce of thug in him. I know he and his mother don't like me very much. I don't know why they don't like me. I mean, I haven't done anything to them. Anyway, I hope to save up enough money to come and visit you one of these days. When I get enough money I'll let you know. I hope you're doing well and I hope that you write me back soon.

Love, Keysha

I filled out an envelope and placed my perfectly

folded letter inside of it. I sealed it and placed it in my duffel bag so that I could mail it in the morning while on my way school.

Early Saturday morning I was sitting next to Jordan in his office. He'd pulled up a bunch of pictures on his computer screen for me to look at. The first photo was of him as a young boy.

"I think I was about six months old in this photo," he said. The photo was of him sitting on a bed holding a bottled filled with milk. The only garment he was clothed in was a white diaper. He was staring directly at the camera when the photo was taken.

"That doesn't even look like you," I said, laughing.

"Well, that's me," he said. He clicked the mouse and another photo popped up. The next photo was of him and his father. They were on the beach. Jordan was standing next to a very large sand castle. His entire body appeared to be covered with brown sand. Also in the photo was another very tall and slim man pointing to Jordan.

"I was about nine years old here. That's your Grandfather Quinton. He and I actually built that sand castle."

"Wow," I said, completely amazed that we had that in common. "What happened to him?" I asked.

"He passed away in his sleep shortly after I graduated from college."

"Are you sad that he's gone?" I asked.

"Yes. He was a good man and I wish you could've known him. He would have loved and spoiled you to death. He loved kids and was a mentor in the church and at the local Boys and Girls Club. Dad was a professor who taught history."

"He sounds as if he was very smart," I said, studying the photo.

"He was the smartest man I've ever known. He loved to read. He'd read anything and the library of books he had was incredible."

"Really?" I got excited. "What happened to all of the books he read?"

"Grandmother Katie has them. When you go visit her I'm sure she'll show them to you."

He clicked the mouse again and another photo came up. This photo was a very old one. It was of an old black man wearing overalls and a hat. He was standing in a prairie field next to two mules.

"Who is that?" I asked, studying the photo. The man's skin looked like soft brown leather.

"That is your great-great-great-grandfather, Roy Tommie."

"He looks worn out," I said.

"Roy Tommie had a hard life, but he did well for a black man during that time period. He was an uneducated but very skilled man. He was a farmer and a carpenter. He helped build houses for emigrants coming in from the Netherlands in the late 1800s. As a young man he worked on an onion farm for a Dutch family who were abolitionists."

"What's an abolitionist?" I asked. I'd heard the word before but I didn't remember exactly what it meant.

"Abolitionists were people who opposed slavery. Have you ever heard of the Underground Railroad?"

"Yeah, sort of. That's the thing where people were running in the middle of the night, right?"

"Something like that. You see, abolitionists were generally people who had a strong belief that slavery was wrong. They helped slaves escape to northern states through a network called the Underground Railroad."

"Oh, okay. I understand now. So, Roy Tommie used to work for these people who were against slavery."

"Yes. Roy Tommie was born into slavery but his family ran away just before the outbreak of the Civil War. He was around six years old at the time. His parents were captured by bounty hunters. He had to survive in the wilderness on his own for five days. He continued to run north until a Dutch abolitionist family named Faulkenberg found him sleeping in their onion field. They took him and kept him well hidden from bounty hunters who came looking for him. After the end of the war, Roy Tommie stayed with the Faulkenberg family, and from them he learned how to become a skilled laborer as well as a farmer. Roy Tommie worked hard and saved up enough money to buy some land from the Faulkenberg family. He built a house on the land he'd purchased and farmed it for years. This is a photo of him around 1925. He was well into his sixties and still farming."

"Wow," I said, completely fascinated by the story. "So what happened to the land and the house?"

"Very good question. It's still in the family. The land has been passed down through the generations, and now Grandmother Katie has a house that's on the land."

"She has all of the land?" I asked, pointing back to the photo.

"No, she doesn't have that much anymore. My grandfather, Willie Curley." He clicked the mouse button again and another photo came up. It was of a man standing, in a suit. He wasn't smiling and looked as mean as the first man.

"In the late 1950s developers wanted the land to build new homes, so Willie Curley sold a large portion of it to them and used the rest of the money to build a new house and put your grandfather and my father, Quinton, through college."

"Wow," I said, feeling a sense of connection. Jordan pulled out a CD and placed it into the CD drive of the computer.

"This CD contains some old eight-millimeter film that I had converted so that I wouldn't lose it. The footage goes back to the 1950s." My dad and I sat there and watched the film. He explained who the people were and what had become of them. I was hungry for more information and more stories. He clicked on a file from the 1980s. When it opened up, a video of my dad with long, greasy hair appeared.

"Oh, hell to the no, you look stupid on this video," I said, laughing as he turned up the sound.

"Hey, back then you weren't cool unless you had a Jerry Curl."

"What are you saying?" I asked, trying to listen carefully to the video.

"I was singing the song 'Rapper's Delight' by the Sugar Hill Gang."

"Oh lord," I said, laughing hysterically as I listened to him try to string all of the words together. "So that's where Mike gets it from," I said, laughing again. I studied the clothes he was wearing.

"What kind of jeans are you wearing?"

"Those are my Sergio Valente jeans. Everyone was wearing them back then. These fashions are still around, you know."

"Why are they so tight?" I asked, but then started cracking up again when I saw him trying to do the pop lock, which I knew as a popular dance from back then. "You couldn't dance, either."

"What are you talking about? I was doing it right." He laughed.

"You're offbeat. Even I can see that—and what's up with those sunglasses?"

"Hey, those sunglasses cost me twenty-five dollars, and I looked good in them."

"You needed fashion help," I said just as the video clip ended. We laughed for a moment, and then I stopped. A feeling of sadness blanketed me. Although Jordan was a complete nerd, he seemed happy. He seemed to have a family who loved and took care of him. I loved my grandmother and mother, but they were con artists and that wasn't cool.

"What's wrong? Why do you look so sad all of a sudden?"

"Can I ask you another question?" I glanced at my hands and began to wring them. I wasn't sure if I wanted to hear the answer to my question.

"Ask," he said.

"How did you find out about me—I mean, why did you even take the blood test? You could've continued on with your life without me." He sighed before he spoke.

"Look at me," he said, but I couldn't. He tilted my chin up and I looked into his eyes. It was hard for me to do that. I felt like what he said next would determine whether I wanted to live or die. Just as he was about to answer my question, Barbara once again barged in on our private time.

"You have to get Mike to his football game. I can't do it," Barbara said. She didn't look at me or acknowledge my presence, and that really irritated me.

"Why can't you do it?" Jordan asked. He seemed surprised by her request as well as her intrusion.

"Hello," I said just so she'd look at me. Our eyes

locked on each other, and I could see utter contempt for me flowing through them.

"Excuse us for a moment, Keysha. Jordan and I need to speak privately."

"What about?" I snapped at her. At that moment I wanted to fight her again. I wanted to scratch up her face and pull all of her hair out. I wanted to hurt her for not giving me time with Jordan.

"Listen you little—" She caught her words.

"Little what?" I sprang to my feet ready to set it off anytime she was ready.

"All right, that's enough. Keysha, excuse us," Jordan said.

"What the hell for?" I yelled out. "I'm tired of her always barging in when I'm trying to talk to you. She doesn't barge in on you when you're talking to Mike and neither do I. So, what's that all about, Barbara?" I worked my neck and pointed my finger in her face. She worked her neck, as well, and was about to say something that I was set to make sure she regretted but Jordan stepped between us.

"Keysha, I'm only going to say it once more. Step out of the office."

"You know what? This isn't working out," I said and left. I went into the family room and found Mike packing his duffel bag.

"What are you looking at?" I barked at him like a vicious dog.

"A little lost ghetto girl," he said and then laughed at me. That did it. I had to put him in his place. I marched into the kitchen and grabbed the wooden broom. I rushed back into the family room howling out like a woman who'd gone mad, and whacked him so hard that the broomstick snapped in half.

chapter 19

W hat's wrong with you, girl? Have you lost your damn mind?" Mike hollered at me as I stood before him with the broken broomstick. He wasn't hurt because of all the football gear he was wearing.

"Say another word and I swear I'll stab you in the neck with this damn broom!" Both of my hands were clutched around the broken broomstick and I desperately wanted him to say something else. I was on edge and was angry enough with him, my situation and the world to do it. At that moment I just didn't care about the consequences of my actions. I just wanted him to give me a reason to kill his spoiled ass.

"Keysha!" Jordan's voice was like a sonic boom in the room. He quickly snatched the broom out of my hand.

"Daddy, that girl is crazy!" Mike squealed like a baby.

"Keysha, go to your room now!" Jordan commanded me.

"He had it coming!" I screamed out. My words were as poisonous as a snake's venom.

"Get up to your damn room before you make me get ugly with you." I looked at the expression on Jordan's face, and I knew he wasn't playing with me. I did as I was told, but in the back of my mind I wanted to kick Mike and his mama's asses for being so mean to me.

I got grounded for a week for attacking Mike. He didn't get in trouble at all for provoking me, and I didn't like that. I felt like he and his mother could get away with treating me like I was Cinderella, and Jordan didn't notice it or refused to notice it. Jordan took away my television and radio. I could have lived without the radio, but the television really hurt.

Sunday night I was in my room because I didn't want to be bothered. I was perfectly fine being by myself because I was used to it. I was lying on my bed with my eyes closed. On the walls of my mind I saw my mother and me. I was visualizing one of the rare times that I was happy to be with her. It was a summer day and it was very hot. My mother and I were on the bus, which was overcrowded with people. I can still smell the stale odor that was wafting through the air. We were going downtown for the Taste of Chicago Food Festival in Grant Park. When we arrived, we walked around all day sampling all types of food. We had ice cream, barbecue turkey legs, pizza, fried

chicken and shrimp gumbo. My stomach was so full that day. At sunset we stood near Buckingham Fountain. It was the very first time I'd seen the fountain. I found a penny on the ground, made a wish and then flicked it into the water. My wish was that my mother would be nice to me all of the time instead of just some of the time.

There was a brief knock on my door and then Mike opened it up. I looked over at him.

"What do you want?" I was still pissed off with him.

"I just wanted to let you know that my father will never love you the way that he loves me."

"Kiss my ashy black ass, Mike," I snapped at him.

"Only in your dreams," he shot back. "By the way, you should know that my mother is working on getting you kicked out of here. She feels that you're a psycho for attacking me with the broom, and I agree with her." He placed a sinister grin on his face and I felt rage flowing through me. I sprang to my feet and raced toward him. Mike quickly turned and ran away from the door just like I knew his punk ass would.

The following day at school I was telling Liz about my situation and how ticked off I was with my stepbrother and stepmother. Liz listened to me vent about it during lunch hour, and I really appreciated her for doing that.

"Do you know what I do when I feel like the world is against me?" Liz asked.

"No, what?"

"I party, girl. I mean, I really party. Sometimes you've just got to do something crazy and insane just to free yourself of all the bullshit that people shovel at you. There is a party at this teen nightclub called Tricked Out that's going on this Friday night. You should come."

"Girl, I'm busted. How am I going to go?" I asked.

"Come on, Keysha, do I have to spell it out for you?"

"What? Sneak out of the house? How am I going to do that?"

"You mean to tell me you haven't figured out how to sneak out of the house yet? Come on, Keysha, you're kidding, right?" Liz asked, surprised that I hadn't mastered the art yet.

"No, I haven't figured it out yet. I just got there," I said, defending myself.

"Okay, let me school you a little. The best way to get out of the house is from your bedroom. Don't walk around the house. You run the risk of waking someone up. Also, don't leave your party clothes in your room. Leave them in the garage inside of a duffel bag. You can change clothes once you get to another bathroom."

"You sound like an old pro at this."

"Let's just say I've learned a trick or two over the years," Liz said as she took a gulp of her soda. I guess she thought that she'd mapped out the perfect plan for me to get out of the house.

"Liz, my bedroom is on the second floor," I said.

"What do you suggest I do? Jump off the damn roof?" I laughed.

"I've done it before," Liz said as if it were no big issue.

"Liz, I'm not about to jump off the roof and possibly break my damn leg in the process."

"Okay, plan B. Act like you've fallen asleep in another part of the house." Something clicked for me at that moment. I remembered that the greenhouse had a door that led outside. I snapped my fingers.

"I just figured a way to get out and back inside the house," I said.

"Cool, then you're going to come to the party, right?"

"Yes," I said, feeling as if I deserved to go out and have a good time. In my mind, I truly believed that. After all I'd been through in the past several months, going out and having a good time was exactly what I needed.

"Now, Liz, there will be cute guys at this club, right?" I wanted to be sure Liz wasn't taking me to some alternative lifestyle hideaway.

"The place is going to be crawling with guys from our school as well as other schools in the area. I'm telling you, Tricked Out is the spot. If you can't pull a guy or girl, depending on how you get down, then you need to go and live in a cave for the rest of your life."

"I am only into boys," I clarified my orientation for her.

"So." Liz leaned in closer to me. "You're not a virgin are you?"

"No," I answered. Liz placed a sinister smirk on her

face. I could tell she was about to fire off a bunch of questions. She wanted to get all up in my sexual history as if she were studying for an exam.

"How old were you when you first did it?"

"Last year when I was fifteen it was my first time."

"You ever give a guy oral sex?" she asked. I guess she thought her question would shock me or make me feel uncomfortable but it didn't. My ex-boyfriend Ronnie and I had done a lot of things.

"Yes," I said, glaring at her. I wanted her to read my facial expressions well. I wasn't afraid of her questions.

"Has a guy ever gone down on you?" she asked.

"Yeah, plenty of times," I answered her. But now I had a question for her.

"My turn," I said. "You ever got down with a girl before?"

"I've done both," she answered.

"So, which do you prefer? Guys or girls?" I wanted to know.

"I consider myself to be bisexual. I like what both sexes can do for me.

"Have you ever been with a girl?" she asked. I placed an angry expression on my face.

"Oh, hell to the no, I just don't get down like that," I answered.

"Have you ever considered it or thought about trying it?" Liz asked, pressing the issue.

I was about to answer with a resounding "no" but I

stopped and thought about the question before I answered. "Well, the thought has crossed my mind but I'd never act on it." Liz smiled at me.

"You're going to have a damn good time at the club Friday night."

"I plan to," I said boldly. At that moment the bell rang and we had to go to our next class. As I walked out into the hallway I thought about going home and standing in front of the mirror so that I could work on my dance moves. After all, it had been a minute since I'd gone out, and the last thing I wanted to do was hit the dance floor looking all stiff. I laughed to myself as I continued on. *I'm going to look hot out on the dance floor. I'm going to burn the memory of my hips and sensual movements into the minds of all the boys at the club.*

When I got home from school, no one was there. I hadn't been in the house a good five minutes when the phone rang. I answered it. It was Jordan.

"I see you made it home," he said.

"Yeah, I'm in here," I answered him.

"Are you okay? You're not afraid are you?"

"No. My mother started leaving me in the house alone when I was eight or nine," I answered him con-descendingly. He was quiet after I said that. I guess he didn't like hearing the truth.

"Okay, Barbara will be there in about a half hour."

"Whatever," I said.

"I want you to work on building a better relation-ship with her," Jordan said.

"I don't see why. She wants me to disappear and you know it." He was silent again for a long moment.

"Listen, if we're going to make this work, we've all got to be willing to put forth an effort."

"I'm not the one you need to be telling this to." I couldn't help speaking my mind to him. I mean, he was coming at me like I was the damn cause of all the drama. I came to the house being as nice as I could be and both Barbara and Mike came at me all twisted.

"We'll talk when I get home," he said and then hung up the phone.

I walked upstairs and noticed that the door to Mike's bedroom was open. I walked toward his room and peeked inside. To my surprise his room was rather clean. In fact, it was too clean. Mike was a neat freak. As I glanced around his tidy room, I noticed that his computer was on. Since no one was home, I decided to see what Web sites he'd been to. I sat down at his computer and hit the button for Internet Explorer. I looked at his fa-vorites list and saw that he had a personal Web page on MySpace. I opened it up and saw that he had a photo of himself without a shirt on. Next to the photo was a little information about him. It said that he was eighteen years old, which was a lie. He listed his city and state correctly. Under the heading "About Me" it read:

Im a gangsta u c. Im Mad funni two. I Lov two go out and party—drinking and smoking ain't my scene-hey I'm doin' my thang, sun. Da Gurlz luv err thang I got, I gotz dat six pac cuz i workout err day. i play football im fine az hell an I keepz ma pockits full of kash. Soo im sayin for all ya cuties out dare if ya think ya can handle da kid holla @ me.

Under the heading of "Favorite Movies" it read, *Scarface, Carlito's Way, Boyz n the Hood* and *Menace II Society.* I noticed that he also had a blog. When I saw that, I felt an exquisite rush of vindictiveness pulse through me. I decided to post a new blog to all of his friends. The title of it was, "I'm a spoiled punk-ass suburban boy who is only thirteen years old."

After I posted a real ignorant blog, I scrolled down to the bottom of his page and peeped that he had close to three thousand friends linked to his page. I decided to click on the first picture that I saw, which was of some guy from Philadelphia. When his page came up, the song, "Hot In Herre" by Nelly began to play. I noticed that he'd posted a video on his page. I clicked another button to turn Nelly off and clicked the button for the video. The boy had videotaped himself dancing in his bedroom without a shirt on. I watched him as he sensually and rhythmically moved to the song "Confessions" by Usher.

"Damn," I said aloud. "He is so fine." I watched the

video several times before I'd had my fill. I copied his Web address and e-mailed it to myself so that I'd be able to find his page again.

I went into my bedroom and shut my door. I pulled out several outfits and finally settled on some Phat Farm jeans and a belly top that exposed my flat and sexy chocolate stomach. I placed the clothes and some accessories in a small duffel bag and rushed out of my room to hide it in the garage so that I'd be able to get it once I'd sneaked out of the house on Friday night. I decided that it would be best to play the role of daddy's little girl and apologize to Jordan and explain that the reason I snapped out on Mike was because I wasn't raised properly. My plans centered on making him feel guilty for not being around during my childhood. I didn't see any harm in using guilt to my advantage. In my mind, I knew that I could pull it off. After all, my mother and grandmother were some of the best con artists around. I wasn't going to mention the party because I didn't want him to get the idea I was pulling one over on him. I wanted him to think I was genuinely sincere, even though I wasn't.

My guilt-trip con worked better than I thought it would. By the end of the week, I had Jordan apologizing to me. It was such a rush to know I'd pulled one over on him. Friday during school, Liz and I mapped out our plan. I told her that I probably wouldn't be able to escape from the house until around eight o'clock in the evening. Once I got out of the house I was to grab my duffel bag and go over to her place. From there we'd head out to the club. I hung out in Jordan's office all evening pretending to read a book. Before he went to bed, he came into his office to say goodnight.

"Are you still reading?" he asked.

"Yup, I love reading. I've never read *Moby Dick* and so far it's really interesting."

"So, what do you think of Captain Ahab?" he asked me. I hadn't actually read the book so I didn't know who the hell Captain Ahab was, but the name sounded crazy as hell, so I took a huge gamble.

"That fool is crazy," I said, smiling at him. I must not have been too far off because he smiled back at me.

"He had an obsession with that whale." He was about to go into details but I stopped him.

"Don't tell me the story, Daddy. Let me read it first," I said, smiling at him really hard. He once again fell for my con, hook, line and sinker.

"You got it," he said. He walked over to me and kissed me on top of my head. "Goodnight," he said and went back upstairs and into his bedroom. I looked at a clock situated on the bookshelf and noticed that it was eight-thirty.

"Damn," I said. "I hope she hasn't left yet." It was hard for me to tell if Liz had given up because Jordan had taken my cellular phone. I had to give it to him when he said that my privileges were going to be taken away for a week, and he meant a full damn week.

* * *

Once I was confident that he and Barbara had gone to bed, I skillfully moved toward the inside greenhouse door. Once I opened it and was inside of the greenhouse, I moved through it quickly and exited out the outer door. I rushed across the driveway to the detached garage. I opened the door, grabbed my duffel bag and rushed off toward Liz's house. Once I was a good distance away from the house, a car pulled up beside me.

"Are you looking for a ride, girl?" I looked to my right and saw Liz driving a black PT Cruiser.

"Girl, where did you get this car?" I asked, walking around to the passenger side. She unlocked the door and let me in.

"Don't worry about it," she answered.

"Do you even have a driver's license?" I asked.

"No, but I drive very well," she said, laughing as we sped off into the night.

"Seriously, Liz. This car isn't stolen, is it?" I asked nervously.

"Now do you honestly think that if I was going to steal a car my first choice would be a goddamn PT Cruiser?"

"Hell, I don't know," I said.

"Well, for the record, if I were going to steal a car, it'd be a Jaguar or something like that," Liz said as she merged over to make a right-hand turn.

"Okay, once again. Where did your crazy ass get this car from?"

"You're such a nervous broad." She chuckled.

"I'm waiting for an answer. I'm not trying to go to jail with you."

"Girl, relax." She placed her hand on my thigh. I looked at her hand and then she removed it.

"It's my car—well, it's really my dad's, but my mother said that I could have it. When I get my license this will be my car. Do you feel better now?" Liz asked.

"Yes, much better," I answered.

"We can go back to my house so you can change clothes."

"What about your mom? Isn't she going to freak out about you driving this car without a license?"

"She's working the night shift and doesn't get home until about one o'clock in the morning. By the time we get back she'll never know that it was even out of the garage."

"What about her boyfriend?"

"What about him? When she works the night shift he hangs out."

About an hour later, Liz and I arrived at the nightclub, which was packed with partygoers. We paid our admittance fee and walked down a long, dimly lit corridor. The walls were painted black and had various concert posters of popular recording artists matted to the walls. Once we arrived at the end of the corridor, we made a sharp left and entered a room as large as our school's gymnasium. Rapper Kanye West's voice was blasting through speakers.

"Come on, let's walk around the club to check out the action." I could barely hear Liz over the noise but I understood her enough to follow her through the dense crowd of people. It was exciting being around all the dancing and music. I felt like I'd been missing out on so much, but I was definitely about to make up for lost time. Club Tricked Out had some seriously fine-looking boys. I felt a lot of eyes on me as I moved around the club, and a few times the boys would get close and whisper things like, "Let me get your number" or "Can we hook up?"

"Look, there is an empty table that we can grab," Liz said as she pulled my hand and led me to the table. Now that I was seated, I looked around and took in the decor in more detail. The bar was on my left. Suspended above the bar was an iron cage with a girl dancing inside of it. She wasn't moving all that well, and I began to think to myself that if I were in there I'd put on a pretty good show. The DJ booth was to my right. Next to the DJ booth was the mechanical bull thrill ride. I watched as some guy tried to hold on for as long as he could until he was tossed safely off onto a heavily padded mat below the machine. Directly in front of me was a large dance floor filled with bodies dancing in wild abandon and brushing against each other sensually. The place was a beautiful spectacle of youth, beauty and untamed energy. You could feel a sense of magic in the air. I was ready to dance and was eager for someone to ask me. Then within a matter of moments a cute boy walked over to where we were sitting.

"I know I'm the one you're looking for," he said as he undressed me with his eyes. I felt a bolt of sensual energy tickle my nerves in the sweetest way.

"What are you? A mind reader or something?" I smiled at him.

"Come on, Keysha, let's dance," Liz said, pulling me away before the guy could even respond back to me.

"Damn, Liz, slow the hell down. That boy was fine," I shouted, but she couldn't really hear me because we were now directly under the speakers. Once I was out on the dance floor, I looked into her eyes and waited for an explanation of her behavior. She drew herself closer to me and spoke purposefully in my ear.

"His girl just walked in with her crew," she said. I looked back in the direction of the cute guy and sure enough he had his arm looped around another girl.

"She and her girls would've been all over you for talking to him. I've seen them in action before," Liz said. "He loves it when his girls fight over him. I almost got into a fight with the girl with the short hair. I could have easily kicked her butt but she backed away."

"Damn, good looking out, girl," I said. "The last thing I need to be involved in tonight is a fight."

"Come on, let's find another seat." Liz and I looped

around the club several times before we finally found a seat near the mechanical bull.

"This placed is packed tonight," Liz said, smiling at me. I smiled back, and for the first time took a good look at what she was wearing. Of course she was wearing all black. She had on a short black skirt with a cute matching black V-neck shirt that hugged her body. Her legs were long and muscular and were in need of a pair of stockings, but Liz still looked attractive.

"Girl, I'm so glad that you told me about this place. I'm going to be here every weekend," I proclaimed as I got caught up in the energy of the atmosphere. I focused my attention back on the dance floor and watched as some girl worked her behind in front of the guy she was with. I could tell he was impressed by the way she moved. I thought I could move better than she could and was looking forward to teasing the imagination of the first cutie who asked me to dance.

"She isn't all that." Liz was apparently looking at the same girl. "She isn't even doing the booty bounce right. It's supposed to go like this." To my surprise, Liz had a whole lot of rhythm for a white girl.

"Girl, where did you learn how to move like that?" I asked with a teasing smile.

"What, you think white girls can't get down? Please, I can do my thing with the best of them." She chuckled. "Hold still for a minute," Liz said as she fixed a strand of my hair that was out of place. "I'm going to get something to drink. Do you want anything?"

"A soda is fine," I said. I was about to give her some money but she quickly told me that she'd pay for it. When Liz stepped away, I turned my attention to the mechanical bull. I watched as a guy and girl rode it together. The girl was holding on to the guy and the guy was holding on to the bull. The machine jerked and twisted them around until they both fell off of it, laughing.

"Do you want to try it?" asked Liz, who had just returned with my drink. I took a few gulps of it before I answered.

"I'd love to try it," I said. "Let me see how much it costs?"

"Don't worry. There is no charge. It's free to ride. Come on, we'll go stand in line." We watched as two other people enjoyed the thrill of the ride.

"Either I'm thirsty as hell or this drink is just damn good," I shouted so that Liz could hear me. I drank the rest of my soda then began to groove to the rhythm of the group Black Eyed Peas.

"Okay, it's your turn. Have fun," said Liz. I took off my shoes and walked out to the bull. I had a hard time mounting the apparatus, but when I finally did I felt a sense of freedom and independence I'd never felt before. Just as I was positioning myself for the ride of a lifetime, Liz hopped on behind me and locked her hands around my waist.

"Liz, what are you doing?" I shouted out but she couldn't hear me. The ride started and I had to hold on. We were spun around in circles and then the bull began shaking violently and I could feel my behind giggling violently. It was an embarrassing, yet wonderful feeling. As we spun around in a different direction I noticed that a bunch of guys were cheering us on.

"Wooooo!" they howled out at the sight of Liz and me riding the bull together. I couldn't help but laugh and smile as Liz clutched my waist harder. I thought for sure I was going to fall off but Liz somehow kept me balanced and on the damn thing. Around and around we went until we were flung off and thrown into the pit. I landed on my back and Liz landed on top of me. We were both laughing hard as the guys continued to shout and howl.

"We gave those guys one heck of a show, now didn't we?" Liz said as she maneuvered herself to her feet, pulled her skirt down and then helped me up.

"No wonder they were howling out. Your underwear was showing," I said.

"And," Liz said as if it were no big deal.

"Never mind," I said, not really caring. I was too busy enjoying the buzzing that was rushing through me. I suddenly felt very alive and as if every nerve in my body was being strummed gently like a harp. It was such a sweet feeling I'd never felt before.

"Girl, that bull ride did something to me," I said as we left the bull pit.

"Yes, it does awaken the senses," Liz admitted. At that moment the song "Bootylicious" by Destiny's Child came blaring through the speakers, and Liz went wild.

"I love this song." She began dancing around slowly and sensually. She moved her body up and made her behind bounce.

"You are so crazy," I said. I looked up at the dancing cage, which was empty, and suddenly I wanted to get inside it and act wild. I wanted to see and tease every guy in the place. I wanted them to see me and want me but not be able to reach or touch me. Without even thinking twice about it, I moved over to the bar and asked to get inside. One of the very muscular and very strong bouncers lifted me up and helped me get inside the cage. He was about to close the door, but then Liz joined me.

"Come on, we're a tag team," she said, and I laughed. I was pleased that she followed my lead and wanted to continue to act crazy and wild.

"You are so insane but I like that about you," I shouted over the noise of the music. We were both lifted up and suspended in the air. I clutched my fists around the bars of the cage and popped and jerked my body and moved like I'd never moved before. I was completely lost in the music, when suddenly I began to feel incredibly aroused. I don't know if it was the exhibition I was putting on or the cheers from all of the guys below glaring up at me. I'd never been so turned on in my life. Then the room seemed to be moving in slow motion. I wanted to be touched so I began to touch my stomach and tug on my clothes as if I were going to take them off in front of everyone. I don't know why, but I felt like a seasoned exhibitionist. The next thing I knew, Liz had placed her hands on my shoulders and I felt as if I was melting. I couldn't believe that I was aroused by a girl's touch. I suddenly felt very confused. I removed her hands from my shoulders and kept dancing. A moment later, Liz placed her hands on my hips and pressed her body against my back. An exquisite sensation washed over me that was both titillating and perplexing. A wisp of her breath blew on my neck, and goose bumps leaped up on my skin. Guys continued to howl out, and I knew that they were enjoying the impromptu show. I glanced down at all the boys and froze up when I saw my brother, Mike. He was glaring at me with eyes that were asking a thousand questions. I gathered myself as best as I could and pushed Liz off me. I felt very strange. I felt as if something wasn't exactly right with the way I was feeling. The way my body was responding to Liz's touch frightened me. I turned around to face Liz. My vision started getting blurry on me. I thought I was about to faint again. Liz was moving very seductively and for some reason her movements started making me feel dizzy.

"Liz," I called to her and she approached me. I wanted to tell her that I wasn't feeling right but my words got trapped in my throat. She thought that I was encouraging her to keep it up. She was all over me, and I felt horrified by it because I liked it. At that moment, I felt as if I was not me. I felt as if I was out of my body looking at myself doing things that I never thought or believed I would do. I finally spoke in Liz's ear.

"I need to get out," I said.

"Why? This is so much fun. Come on, you're into it," she said and kept dancing. Thankfully the song was ending and we were let back down. Once we were back on solid footing, Liz said, "Woo, girl, you're so hot!" She was glancing at me as if she wanted to kiss me. I didn't understand myself at that moment.

"I need a drink," she said and excused herself. I found an empty seat and sat down. My brother came up to me.

"What are you doing here? You're grounded until tomorrow." I just looked at him with an incoherent glare.

"When Dad finds out he is going to go through the roof. You're so busted," he said. I could hear his words but I felt as if I had trouble fully understanding him. Something was definitely out of place. I touched him, and his skin felt really silky. It was a wonderful feeling.

"Wow, you have such soft skin," I said. Mike studied me for a long moment.

"You are so smashed," he said. "What are you on?" he asked, but I couldn't answer him. At that moment I only wanted to find Liz. I was missing her and needed to know her whereabouts.

"Where is Liz?" I asked. Mike didn't answer me.

"You need to leave," he said.

"Where in the hell is Liz!" I shouted at the top of my voice.

"I don't know," he said. I got up and walked around to search for her. I don't recall how long I'd been walking or at exactly what point I exited the club, but somehow I ended up sitting on the hood of someone's car. I placed my face in my hands to try and pull myself together. I was having difficulty remembering why I came outside in the first place. I got up and started walking deeper into the parking lot.

"Hey, baby, you looking for a party?" I heard someone behind me ask. I turned around and there were three guys glaring at me.

"What party?" I foolishly asked.

"We're having a party right here in the parking lot," he said. I didn't care about his party. I only wanted to find Liz, so I began walking again. Off in the distance I saw two silhouettes. One silhouette appeared to be strangling or choking the other figure.

Whoa, I thought to myself as I tried to wrap my thoughts around what my eyes were seeing.

"Did you get the job done?" I heard a male voice ask as I got closer.

"Yes," I heard a female voice say. I think it was Liz.

"Come on, girl, you want to party with us." The guy grabbed my arm and started pulling me away.

"Am I supposed to go with you?" I asked. My mind was in a fog. "Liz, baby, why did you leave me in there? Don't you know how much I need you?"

"Yeah, girl, my name is Liz. That's right, keep calling me Liz." I heard a bunch of guys laughing.

"What's so funny?" I asked, but before I could get an answer I collapsed.

"Damn it. It's the first day on my new legs," I said.

"Open your legs," I heard a male voice say.

"Why?" I asked. I managed to get back to my feet. I couldn't see clearly and my vision was very blurry. I started walking again but I'd only taken about three steps and collapsed to the ground again between two cars. For some reason the ground felt as soft as a pillow and I was suddenly sleepy. I lay down and rested. I last thing I remember was someone yelling, "Get away from her!"

chapter 20

When I woke up, I was in my bed fully clothed, and I had no idea of how I'd gotten there or why I was sleeping with all of my clothes on. I felt as if someone was inside my head smashing the walls of my skull with a sledge hammer. I had a migraine headache that was out of this world. As I became more aware of my surroundings, I could hear muffled voices arguing.

"What in the world happened to me?" I said aloud as I sat up in my bed. I looked around my room and, for a brief moment, I recalled sneaking out of the house to hang out with Liz. I knew that we went out, but the last thing I remembered was riding the mechanical bull with Liz. All of my other memories were very vague and unclear. The urge to puke was strong so I got out of bed and made my way to the toilet just in time. I remained on my knees puking for a good five minutes. I felt as if I'd been kicked in the gut by an angry horse.

* * *

"You know, I've never heard them fight like this before. If my parents get a divorce because of you, I swear I'll kill you my damn self," Mike said angrily.

"Get away from me, Mike, I'm not in the mood today," I said as I tried to remember what day it was. I puked again. I scratched my scalp with my fingertips and tried to remember what happened. I kept seeing flashes of myself riding the bull with Liz, but nothing more. I moved over to the faucet and turned it on so that I could wash my face and brush my teeth.

"You do realize how very wrong things could have gone for you last night?" Mike asked.

"Gone wrong?" I asked, confused.

"Last night," he said as if I should've known. "You don't remember, do you?"

"Remember what?" I looked at him, confused. There was a long moment of silence between us.

"What do you think happened to you?" he asked. He appeared to be fascinated with me for the moment.

"I know that I went out with Liz. I'm assuming that I snuck back in the house and was so tired that I didn't take off my clothes," I said. It sounded like the most logical explanation. I looked into his eyes and saw that my account of events was way off. I suddenly felt as if I were in a dream, falling backward into darkness.

"Aww, man, you were so fried, you don't even remember what you were doing?" Mike had a perplexed look on his face. "You have no idea of how much trouble you've gotten yourself into or how you—"

"You can't scare me, Mike, so don't even try it," I interrupted him. My stomach started doing flips and I had to puke once more.

"Here, let me help you," Mike said, handing me a warm face cloth.

"Thanks," I said.

"You looked like you were doped up last night."

"Doped up? What the hell are you talking about? I don't do drugs."

"Sure, you don't do drugs." Mike didn't believe that I was telling him the truth. "Whatever you were on, it had you all whacked out. I'm the one who brought you home and Dad is the one who put you in bed. You were so out of it that you thought Dad was Estelle."

"Estelle," I said, wondering why I would have thought that.

"I think you were hallucinating. By the way, who is Estelle?"

"My aunt. She passed away earlier this year."

"Oh, sorry to hear that."

I paused in thought for a moment as I tried to remember what happened to me. Again, I could only see quick flashes of what had gone down. I did remember feeling very aroused, and I didn't understand why.

"Mom and Dad know about you sneaking out of the house and your dope problem."

"I don't have a dope problem," I said as I exited the bathroom.

"Yes, you do, and you'd better get help for it because that just isn't cool." Mike didn't say anything else. He just went into his bedroom and shut the door. I began walking down the stairs but stopped midway so I could sit and listen to Jordan and Barbara argue about me.

"You gave it a shot, okay. I'll give you credit for trying to correct a mistake, but at this point you have to toss in the towel, Jordan."

"She needs help, Barbara. She doesn't need another person to turn their back on her," Jordan argued.

"You can't save her, Jordan. She's too far gone. If she stays in this house, she's going to ruin everything we've worked so hard for. She has to go."

"And where do you suggest she goes? She has no other family."

"I don't care where she goes as long as she leaves this house. We can call that social worker back and tell her that we tried but we can't deal with her. Let her go back to the group home until her mother can come for her."

"Barbara, I'm not sending her back there. She's been through enough already," Jordan countered.

"And what about us? Huh? What about what she's putting Mike and me through? She's using drugs, Jordan. My God, are you fully comprehending what this means? We're going to have to hide all of the valuables. She may let her drug dealer break into our home. Anything could happen."

"I know that she has some problems, but I felt as if I was getting through to her. I felt like we were able to connect last week. She's a part of me, Barbara, and I can't change that."

"She's playing you for a complete fool, Jordan, and you're too damn blind to see it."

"I'm not blind," he snapped back.

"Jordan, she acted nice to you all week so that you'd let your guard down, that's all. I'll bet you she planned how she was going to manipulate you in order to sneak out of the house."

"She wouldn't do that to me," I heard him say.

"She already has, Jordan."

"Look, I'm going to put a special lock on the basement doors so that she can't sneak out at will. There are going to be severe consequences for what she's done, but I'm also going to look into getting her some help."

"Why don't we just send her back, Jordan?" I could tell that Barbara was pleading with him.

"Because it's not her fault. It's my fault," he answered. I was like, whoa, when I heard that one. I couldn't believe that he actually felt that responsible for me.

"If she does one more thing, Jordan, I swear to you, our marriage is going to suffer because of it."

The next thing I heard was hard footsteps and a door

slamming. I swallowed hard and then stood up. I wanted to defend myself and let Jordan know that I didn't do drugs and how I didn't understand what had happened to me. It was the first time that I really wanted to open up to him and explain myself. Hell, I even wanted to apologize to him for manipulating him just as Barbara knew I had. I'd never seen nor heard anyone stand up for me like Jordan had.

I walked down the rest of the stairs and into the kitchen. I stood at the archway between the kitchen and the family room and stared at my father. He was sitting down on the sofa glaring directly at me. His eyes were red with rage, his jaw was tight and his chest was still heaving from the confrontation he'd just had with Barbara. I wanted to tell him that there was just a big misunderstanding about me and that I didn't mean for things to happen the way that they had. I tried to speak but my words wouldn't come out of my mouth. My father's hardened gaze put the fear of God in my heart. I felt that at any moment he was going to snap at me in a way that would scar me emotionally for the rest of my life.

"Go back to your room and don't come back down here until I tell you to."

"But—"

Jordan sprang to his feet, rushed over to me and locked his hand around my wrist. He hauled me back through the kitchen into the dining room to the staircase.

"This is not a damn game I'm playing!" His voice

roared like thunder and was filled with hell's fury. It was the very first time that I felt afraid of him. I began to cry as I rushed back upstairs to my room. I wished that there was a way I could explain everything and make him believe that I was telling him the truth.

chapter 21

I didn't have any appetite, so I didn't eat dinner that night. I remained in my room and started reading *Moby Dick* to escape from the pain I'd caused. The next morning I woke up very early. I was awake before anyone else in the house. I opened my door to go to the bathroom but stopped when I saw an envelope sitting outside of my door. I reached down to pick it up and saw that a letter from my Grandmother Rubylee had arrived. I went back inside my room and shut the door. I sat down on my bed, ripped the envelope open and read her letter.

Dear Keysha,

It has taken me a while to get my thoughts together enough to write you. Prison life isn't easy, but I'm making the best of it. I'm working on my getting out of here so that I can have my freedom back. The prison guards in here aren't very nice, and the food is nasty. At night I sleep on a hard bed with bedsheets that have a sour odor. The bedsheets smell like they've been inside of a Dumpster filled with spoiled food. Adding to my misery are the large spiders that chew on me all night while I'm asleep. Sometimes I don't sleep at all. I just stare up at the ceiling and try to make myself believe I'm not in here. The prison guards tried to break my spirit but I won't let them. I'm too strong, too smart and too tough for that to happen.

I was trying to think of things you'd want to know about my life as it is now. The best I can do for you is to describe a typical day and what it's like on the inside of this place. I'm not in a prison cell like you see on television. I'm in a dorm room setting. Everyone is in a big room with a mattress and a locker. You can't hang any posters or pictures because the walls are solid white brick. The floor isn't carpeted, it's gray and made of concrete. Let me tell you, it gets bone-chilling cold in here during the winter. Prison is supposed to be about rehabilitating a person so that they can go out and function in society. However, I've run into more corruption in here than I ever did out on the streets. I've got myself a little trading hustle going on in here. One of the girls in the stockroom and another one in the cafeteria used to run the streets with me back when I was messing around with Stanback. I'm not sure if you remember Stanback. He was your grandfather but he was killed a long time ago. Anyway, my girl in the supply room makes sure that I get extra toiletries in my weekly care package so I can trade them for cigarettes *or other things I may need. Believe it or not, you only get one roll of toilet paper every seven days. If you run out before then you're up shit's creek without a paddle. So women come to me when they need hygiene products and I give my girls a percentage.*

When I wake up in the morning I have at least two or three women putting in orders with me. When I go to the cafeteria for breakfast, I give my order to my girl who is serving food and she gets it to my girl in the supply room who then makes sure that my weekly toiletry bag is filled with all of the right stuff.

After breakfast I head to the break room where I sit and talk to people while playing cards or some other game to take my mind off of where I'm at. Around one o'clock we get an hour of free time out in the prison yard. I mostly walk around and talk to people but you have to be careful about that because not everybody around here gets along. You could easily end up in a fight and if you get jammed up you have to go to a hearing in front of a prison judge who then disciplines you by adding time to your sentence. So far, I've had four altercations and I've had seven months added on to my time. I've taken on the meanest and baddest women in this place and have whipped them all. You can't walk around this place with fear in your eyes because the women in here will take advantage of you. From two o'clock to six o'clock, I'm in the library shelving books. The small amount of money I make is placed on the prison books. The money is supposed to help me start over when I get out. It's nice doing that type of work but I don't think it's going to serve me well when I get out of here. I just do it to pass the time. After that I go back to the cafeteria and eat dinner, which isn't very good. After dinner they usually have a movie for us to watch, and then after that I go back to my locker and fill my orders. After that's done, I lie on my back and try not to let the spiders chew on me.

I'm not sure how you found out who your real daddy is. Your mama was out running the streets with so many guys during the time she got pregnant. It sounds like your father is a good, quality man with some money. Money is what makes the world go around, Keysha, even in prison. So when you do come to see me make sure you have some money for me. In fact, I want you to send me any allowance money that you get so that it can be put on the books for me. Since you're living in high society now, I know you can afford to send your Grandmother Rubylee some money. In fact, I know I shouldn't be writing this because sometimes the guards read your mail, but I'm going to risk it. Look around your daddy's house and see if you can find his bank account information as well as his social security number. If you can get that information to me, I know some people who can make sure that you and I both can reap all of the benefits of a man with good credit.

Let me know when you're coming my way.
Your Grandmother,

Rubylee

* * *

I was sick after I read her letter. I couldn't believe she had the nerve to ask me to rip off my own father. I buried my face inside my pillow and screamed as loud as I could before I began crying.

chapter 22

As I walked through the hallway to my locker on Monday morning, guys were gawking at me, and I didn't know why. I couldn't wait to see Liz so I could find out what I did, because I still couldn't remember much. I didn't see Liz in the hallway but thought for sure I'd see her in our first-period math class. When I walked into our math room, one of the students, named Lou Lopez, spoke to me.

"What's up, cage bird?"

"What's that supposed to mean?" I wasn't in the mood for any nonsense.

"Let's just say I now know why the caged bird sings." He along with several other students laughed at me, and I didn't know why. I didn't like being ridiculed because it didn't feel good at all. I didn't see Liz at all during the day so I assumed that she didn't come to school. I couldn't call her because my phone privileges had been completely taken away.

After school I had to go to the football stadium and sit in the bleachers and wait for Mike to get done with football practice so we could walk home together. Since my parents didn't trust me, I couldn't enter the house without Mike. When practice was over I walked home with Mike, who refused to speak to me. He'd recently checked his MySpace account and realized that I'd posted a very mean-spirited blog about him.

When I first posted it I didn't feel bad at all, but after learning that he actually made sure that I got home safely Friday evening, I felt like crap for doing what I did.

"Mike, I said I was sorry. How many times do you want me to apologize to you?" I asked. Mike didn't say anything, he just kept walking in front of me as if I didn't exist. When we got to the house he immediately went to the phone and called Jordan to let him know that we were both safely in the house. Mike was now my personal watchdog who was just itching for me to screw up again so that he could tell Jordan and Barbara. I went into the family room with my duffel bag, sat down on the sofa and removed my homework from the bag. Mike came into the family room and turned on the television. News reporter Angela Rivers was supplying the known details about several teenagers who became very ill after taking the hallucinogenic drug Ecstasy while at the Tricked Out teen dance club.

"Police officials are saying at this time several Thornwood High School students had to be transported to area hospitals for treatment. One of those students is said to have suffered brain damage from taking the drug," said the reporter.

"Did you hear that?" I asked Mike but he didn't acknowledge me.

"Police are saying that there is an ongoing investigation as to how students obtained the illegal drug. Police are working with the school and school district officials. We'll be reporting more on this story as the details become clearer." As Angela Rivers concluded her report, Mike glanced at me for a long moment, but didn't say a word. I could see the suspicion in his eyes.

"What?" I asked.

"I hope you're not involved in that mess," he said.

"I'm not," I quickly answered. "I don't know anything about that." I was insulted so I gathered up my belongings and went upstairs to my room.

The following morning at school, I was removing my science book from my locker when Liz finally surfaced.

"Hey, girl, I have something for you," Liz said, returning my duffel bag to me from Friday evening. I took it and stuffed it inside my locker.

"Where have you been?" I asked.

"Hell, I felt like ditching school so I did," she answered as if it were no big deal.

"What the hell happened to you Friday night? Why did you leave me?"

"Leave you? Huh, that's a laugh. You disappeared on

me." At that very moment I remembered going out into the parking lot to search for her.

"No, I went looking for you, Liz." My memory was still kind of hazy.

"What's going on, love birds?" Lou Lopez teased us as he walked by. I glared at Lou with hate as he passed.

"Ooh, what's that nasty look for?" Liz asked. I focused my attention back on her.

"Look at you," Liz said, adjusting a loose strand of my hair. I didn't like her touching me and she must have sensed it. "Come on, don't be like that. You were so into it Friday night."

"Into what? I swear I barely remember anything that happened that night. Then on the news I heard about students who got sick because someone was passing around Ecstasy. My father doesn't trust me, my stepmother hates me, my brother despises me, my mother is in jail and my Grandmother Rubylee wants me to rip off my dad and take him for everything he's got. I swear, my life is so screwed up right now that I don't know what to do."

"Jeez, look on the bright side. At least the cops aren't searching the school looking for you."

"Why would they be?" I asked as I exhaled and slammed my locker shut.

"The police are here doing an investigation involving that Ecstasy scandal," Liz said. She tried to touch me again but I moved.

"I don't like it when you do that, Liz."

"What? I didn't do anything." She laughed at me as if she didn't take me seriously.

"Whatever," I said and headed toward our science class. As soon as we sat down the teacher announced that there was going to be a pop quiz.

Damn it, I thought to myself, *I haven't been following along or keeping up with reading the textbook like I was supposed to at all.*

"It's okay, we can flunk it together," Liz said. I just rolled my eyes in annoyance at her. She didn't seem to care about what I was going through, and I didn't understand why. I mean, when she was talking about how much she missed her dad, I was there for her, but now that I have a problem, she thinks my situation isn't important. As I looked at the questions on the test I knew right away that I was going to flunk it because I didn't know any of the answers. I didn't have even the slightest clue because I had a "who gives a damn" kind of attitude, just like Liz. As I sat there staring at the page, the principal and two uniformed police officers walked into the classroom. My heart began to pound and I didn't know why. Liz was summoned to go with them and my heart damn near stopped. Liz captured my gaze as she got up. Her eyes were asking a thousand questions that I didn't know the answers to. Liz never returned to class. I thought I'd see her in our next class but I didn't. There were reports and rumors all around the school about how the police and the principal were pulling students out of their classes. Then, during my lunch hour they came for me.

"Keysha Kendall," I heard an officer call my name just as I was about to sit down. I swallowed hard.

"Yes," I answered him.

"You have the right to remain silent. Anything you say can and will be used against you in a court of law." *Oh, damn, I'm being arrested, but for what? What did I do?* I felt a panic attack consume me. I began to breathe hard and wring my hands.

"What's going on?" I asked.

"You're under arrest," said an officer as he removed his handcuffs. I felt dizzy, and the next thing I knew I fainted.

chapter 23

Fainting didn't help my situation at all, because once I was revived, I was placed under arrest and taken to the principal's office. I was so nervous that my bottom lip trembled uncontrollably. I wanted to call my mother but I couldn't. I could've called Jordan but I was too afraid to because he was so angry with me, and I knew that an episode like this would land me back at the group home for sure. I knew that Barbara would see to it this time. The two police officers left me in the care of my guidance counselor, Mr. Sanders, while they went and searched for another student.

"Keysha, you're in some very serious trouble," said Mr. Sanders. "This is what the police found in your locker once it was opened." He pointed to a large clear plastic bag with a load of pills in it.

"That's not my bag," I said.

"It was in your locker, Keysha. How did it get there?"

"I don't know but that's not my bag or pills." Mr. Sanders exhaled slowly and looked at me with judgmental eyes. I read his facial expression and knew right away that he didn't believe me one bit.

"Look, I'm just trying to help. Just tell me where you got it from?"

"I'm telling you that I don't know," I shouted at him. He picked up a file from his desk and opened it up. He didn't say anything for a long moment.

"So your mother has been arrested and is currently serving time until her court date. Your grandmother was arrested and convicted of bank robbery and—"

"Don't you bring them into this," I snapped at him. "I am not them, and I don't appreciate you trying to insinuate that I'm a criminal, because I'm not."

"Okay, Keysha. Have it your way. The police have returned, anyway. I've tried to help you but I can't if you are unwilling to help yourself."

"Her locker is the only one that had the drugs in it," said one of the officers.

"That's not my stuff," I told him.

"Does anyone else have the combination to your locker?" asked the officer.

"No," I answered him.

"Then how did this bag of drugs get in there?"

"I don't know—I have no clue." I wanted him and everyone to believe me but I saw by their expressions that they didn't.

"Come on," said one of the officers who helped me stand up. I was then escorted out of the building between classes so everyone saw me. I was placed in the backseat of the squad car, and hauled off to the police station.

Once I arrived at the station I was taken into an interrogation room for further questioning and processing. The interrogation room was very small with solid white brick walls. It reminded me of the room my Grandmother Rubylee described in her letter. There were no posters, no artwork or anything of that sort on the walls to give the room any life. The room felt like a tomb, and the police officers were there to seal my fate.

The police officials left me in the room all alone for a long time. I was a little feisty when I'd arrived because I knew that I was innocent and that all of this was some huge misunderstanding. They left me alone in my tomb until I calmed down. I felt as if I had no one I could depend on. I felt as if no one would come to defend me or speak up for me. I began to think about my Grandmother Rubylee's letter and how she described prison life. I felt my tears swelling up because I didn't want to go to jail. My body just started trembling all of a sudden and I couldn't control it. I felt as if I were coming unglued. I felt as if my mind couldn't take or comprehend what was going on.

In all honesty, I felt as if I'd just reached my crossroads. I could turn left and go down the crazy road or turn right and try to fight to prove my innocence. At that moment, the crazy route was the road I was leaning toward. In my mind, it offered me a sense of peace that I wouldn't get anywhere else. I wouldn't have to talk to anyone and I would be able to live inside of my own world, with my own rules and laws. At the very moment I was about to make my choice, I heard the door open. I looked over my shoulder and saw my father. Never in my life had I been so happy to see him, even if he did have a crazy look on his face.

"Daddy?" I said, bursting into tears. I couldn't help it. I stood up, locked my arms around his neck and buried my face in his shoulders. I was so happy to see him. I was so happy to know he cared enough to come when I thought he wouldn't. Jordan hugged me back, and being held by him for the very fist time made me feel safe.

"I didn't do it, Daddy," I said through my tears. "This is all some big mix-up."

"All right, we'll get this all sorted out," he assured me. "First I need you to calm down, okay?"

"I just want to go home with you," I said, refusing to unlatch myself from his embrace. "Please take me home," I pleaded. "Please make them leave me alone." Jordan didn't say anything, he just stroked my hair and kissed the top of my head. I cried some more. I didn't realize I had so many emotions stored up inside of me. I cried so much that I wet up the front of his suit.

"I'm sorry," I said as I finally lifted my face. He wiped

the tears away from my cheeks, and we locked our eyes on each other. I wanted to tell him that I loved him. I wanted him to know that deep in my heart I truly loved him for taking the test and saving me from the group home, but a boulder was in my throat blocking my words.

"I'm going to ask you this one time and I want a straight answer. I don't care if you're guilty or innocent. All I want is the truth." I felt more tears surfacing, but I didn't take my eyes off of him.

"Were you planning to sell and distribute Ecstasy to the students at your school?"

"No, Daddy, I wasn't." My voice trembled. I could feel my lips quivering as I found the strength to answer him.

"Have you ever used or been addicted to any type of drug?"

"No, Daddy, I've never used anything. My mother and grandmother did a lot of things that just turned me off. I never wanted to be like them. I've always wanted a better life for myself, and I never thought I could until you came into my life." He searched my eyes and face for the truth.

"That is the truth, Daddy," I said, still looking him directly in the eyes. "I don't know how that stuff got inside of my locker."

"Okay, I have an attorney on the way. We'll get through this," he said.

"Do you believe me?" I asked, because I needed to know. I wanted and needed him to know that I wasn't using or manipulating him in any way.

"I'm your father, and whether you're right or wrong, I'll always be here for you," he said. "And yes, I do believe you."

chapter 24

Several hours later, I learned that I was being charged with possession of a controlled substance with the intent to distribute it. Asia, a woman of Chinese descent whom my father went to undergrad school with, was the attorney he hired. Asia informed us that it was going to be a long, hard fight, especially if the batch of Ecstasy found in my locker was linked to the batch that caused a severe reaction in the people at the Tricked Out dance club. And especially since one kid actually got brain damage from the stuff.

"If she's found guilty, you should expect a civil lawsuit from the parents of the child with brain damage to follow," said Asia.

"But I didn't do it. That's not my stuff," I said.

"I know and I believe you. We just have to make a judge believe you. We do have several things in our favor. You don't have any criminal history and there is no medical file that indicates you've had addiction problems. I'm going to be honest with both of you. The prosecution is under pressure to bring someone to justice. Apparently, according to police, there has been a recent invasion of Ecstasy in this community, and they want to stop it."

"But I don't even know where to get the stuff," I said.

"That's another thing. The prosecution contends that they have a witness who says that they saw you with a man named Trinity Neophus Friday night at Tricked Out. Police say he has strong ties to the drug world."

"I have no clue as to who that is. And whoever this witness is they've found is flat-out lying."

"Were you at this club last Friday evening?" asked Asia.

"Yes, I was there, but I don't remember everything that happened. I got sick and fainted. My brother had to bring me home."

Asia exhaled. "Look, we're free to leave now. Bail has been posted, and we'll be notified of a court date in the coming weeks. Keysha, it is very important that you don't talk to anyone other than me, your father or mom about this case. Anything that you mention to friends at school can be used against you in court."

"So I need to keep my mouth shut about all of this?" I asked.

"Yes. And under no circumstances should you speak with the media. That's my job as your attorney."

"Okay," I said, feeling as if I'd somehow gotten myself into something that was way over my head.

When we arrived home it was around six-thirty in the evening. No sooner had we set foot in the house, than Barbara began snapping out on Jordan.

"Do you see now, Jordan? She's too much," Barbara began talking about me. Before, she would at least wait until I was in another room, but now she just didn't care whether I heard what she said or not. "This girl is going to rip us apart!"

Jordan sat down on the sofa in the family room. Now I wanted to be there for him. I wanted to defend and fight for him the way he'd done for me.

"I'm not trying to rip you apart," I said. Barbara's eyes became slits in her face.

"Listen, you little—"

"That's enough, Barbara," Jordan cut her off. She took her attention off me and focused back on Jordan. I went and sat down next to my daddy.

"We are going to stick together on this," Jordan said. "We're going to get through this storm—"

"You believe her, don't you?" Barbara had a shocked expression on her face. "Jordan, how can you be so blind?"

"I'm telling the truth," I said, hoping she'd understand.

"Okay, hang on a minute," Barbara said. She marched

out of the room and returned with the letter that Grandmother Rubylee had written me. "I didn't want to have to do this but I guess you have to see it for yourself." She handed him the letter. "Read the highlighted part." Jordan looked down at the letter. I glanced over at it and saw that Barbara had highlighted Rubylee's request for money and bank account information.

"Do you see now, Jordan? The girl and her grandmother are plotting to clean us out! For all we know, Rubylee could be running a narcotics ring from prison, and if we're linked to it we could lose everything. The house, our lifestyle, everything!"

"Grandmother Rubylee is crazy, okay?" I said because I didn't want my daddy to think I was playing some kind of game with him.

"Why would she ask you to do something like this?" Jordan asked me. I looked into his eyes and saw nothing but pain.

"Daddy, I don't know. All I told her was that I'd found you and that you had a nice house."

"Well, now she has our address and can probably send a hit squad or something over here to take us all out," Barbara insisted. She was very passionate about her position.

"It's not like that at all," I said. "You have everything all twisted."

"Keysha, I want you to go upstairs while Barbara and I talk."

"Yeah, get upstairs, because you have a lot of work to do." Barbara's anger toward me was teetering on turning into violence.

"Come on, let's go take a ride," I heard Jordan say to Barbara.

When I got upstairs, Mike was waiting for me on the landing. We locked eyes for a moment. He didn't say anything and neither did I, but I could tell that at that moment he didn't like me very much.

"My life was sweet until you came along," he finally said. "Why are you doing this to us?"

"I didn't do anything, Mike," I said sincerely.

"I've never seen my mom go so crazy," he said, pointing to my bedroom. I looked down the hall toward my bedroom. It looked as if a tornado had gone through it.

"What did she do?" I asked as I rushed into my bedroom.

"She really lost it when she found out about drugs being found in your locker. She demolished your bedroom," Mike said. My bedroom was a complete disaster. Every dresser drawer had been pulled out and dumped out. All of my clothes were turned inside out, and all of the pockets were hanging out of them. She even cut open my mattress and pulled out the foam. As my mind processed all of this I felt weak. I placed my back against the door frame and slid down to the floor. I closed my eyes, and placed my face in my hands.

"Why is my life such a mess?" I spoke aloud. "Why can't things ever go right for me?"

chapter 25

The following day I didn't go to school because I'd been suspended. I didn't sleep well, my stomach was sour and I felt as if I were coming down with the flu. Around midmorning I turned on the television to catch the news and to my surprise and horror, reporter Angela Rivers was doing a follow-up story on the Ecstasy problem in my neck of the woods.

"Tonight school board officials in District 411 will have to face residents who are angered and outraged that the student charged with possession of the drug Ecstasy has only been suspended and not expelled from the school. Many residents say that their quiet close-knit suburban community now has a black eye because of the drug scandal, and many of them are not happy about it."

Angela paused briefly while video interviews played of residents talking about how they wanted school officials to get rid of any student who was involved in any way with the drugs. My heart began to beat very fast and I began to panic and hyperventilate. I couldn't believe how serious the residents were about kicking me out of the neighborhood.

The school board meeting begins at seven o'clock tonight, and many of the residents I spoke with said they planned to be there to express their views and concerns.

Angela concluded her report, and I turned off the television. I now felt sicker than I ever had before.

That evening I sat in the family room with Mike and watched the school board meeting on our local community cable channel. The meeting was held inside the high school cafeteria, and it was packed with parents and students from not only my high school but other high schools within my district. I watched as they talked about issues regarding building repairs, school supplies and funding for extracurricular activities. Everything seemed to be going fine and no one mentioned anything about the drug problem until they reached a part on the agenda that called for open comment. Then, all hell broke loose. Parents were yelling at the board members about protecting their children. One person even wanted random searches of student lockers. Then some lady stood up and attacked Barbara directly.

"Mrs. Kendall, I've heard that this drug problem didn't seem to appear until your stepdaughter began attending Thornwood High School. It is also rumored that she is the one actually behind all of this. In light of this, don't you think it would be wise for you to step down as school board president?" My heart dropped when I heard that lady ask such a mean question.

"Oh, go to hell, lady," Mike shouted at the television screen.

"Why would she ask a question like that?" I asked Mike. I didn't like Barbara very much but I certainly didn't wish for her to be put on public display. In my mind I knew that she was going to say something negative about me and I didn't know if I could take hearing it. Barbara repositioned herself in her seat before speaking into the microphone.

"To place such a heavy blame on my stepdaughter would be unfair. Let's keep in mind that what you've heard are only allegations. She has not and never has been convicted of a crime."

"So are you saying that she didn't have the drugs in her locker?" The woman pressed the issue.

"No, what I'm saying is you're asking me about a personal situation with my family that I feel is inappropriate to bring up at this meeting."

"Get her, Momma," Mike shouted out. It was the first time that I realized just how strong Barbara was.

"However, to ease your concerns I will tell you that I believe my stepdaughter has been wrongly accused and that I do not believe she has or ever did intend to become a dope pusher. My family and I stand united with her, and we will have our day in court where her innocence will be proven beyond a shadow of a doubt."

"That's right, Mama, you tell them. They just can't push us around." Mike continued to taunt the television. My jaw hit the floor. I couldn't believe Barbara actually defended me. I was speechless and didn't know what to think. I looked at Mike, who pressed the mute button on the television.

"So do you believe me?" I asked him.

"My mom went through your bedroom like a mad woman. She thought for sure she'd find a hidden stash of something, but she didn't. This morning on my way to school she shared a family secret that I never knew about. Her older sister used to be on drugs, and she watched how it destroyed her and my grandparents. Eventually she got help, but not until after a whole lot of emotional damage. Anyway, she was glad that she didn't find anything. The fact that she didn't gave you credibility in her eyes. You have to understand something, Keysha. I may have been mean to you but I never wanted any harm to come to you. Even after you hit me with the broomstick, I wasn't mad at you because

I knew that I had it coming. When I saw you at the dance club I knew something wasn't right. You weren't yourself at all. After you left me I tried to find Liz because I wanted to know what the deal was. I wanted to know why you were acting so differently. When I couldn't find her I started searching for you again. One of the guys on the football team told me you were out in the parking lot and several guys were taunting you. By the time I got back out there with the guys, you had fallen to the ground and they were about to have their way with you. That just wasn't cool. Even if I did fight with you all the time, I wasn't going to stand by and watch them violate you."

Mike paused in thought and I suddenly saw him as a completely different person. He'd actually come to my rescue when I needed help. Now that I was thinking clearly, I saw that the entire family was standing by my side. No one was going to leave me hanging.

"Thank you," I said and remained quiet for a moment. "What about you? Do you believe me?" I held my breath as I awaited his answer.

"Yeah, I believe you," he said as he turned the volume back up. I wanted to hug him. I wanted him to know that it meant a great deal to me to have his support.

"I'm so lucky to have a kid brother like you," I said. I draped my arm over his shoulder and gave him a big hug. It felt so good to have a family who cared about me. I wanted to cry again, but I didn't because I knew

Mike would think that I was way too emotional. I enjoyed that moment we had with each other and looked forward to having more of them because I knew that I'd need them, especially once the trial began.

chapter 26

Shortly after dinner I went upstairs to my bedroom, which was still messed up from Barbara's tirade. I started picking up a few of my belongings but stopped because the clean-up job was overwhelming. Instead, I rested on my bed, which wasn't very comfortable but I still tried to find a good position that didn't feel too awkward. As I relaxed on my back with my eyes closed, the image of being handcuffed and taken to jail kept flashing in my mind. I thought I'd fall asleep easily but that just wasn't the case because my mind wouldn't shut off. Another image of a judge slamming down a gavel and saying, "You're guilty," kept replaying itself. Even though I knew I was innocent I felt that I was hexed and everything that could go wrong would go wrong during the trial and I would be hauled off to jail for a crime I didn't commit. I attempted to calm my nerves by taking several deep breaths but it had no impact whatsoever on my paranoia.

After tossing around and slapping my forehead with the palm of my hands a few times, I developed a headache and concluded that no matter how hard I tried, my bed just wasn't going to feel right. I decided to go into the spare room and sleep on Grandmother Katie's bed. Once I entered her bedroom, I relaxed my tortured body on her soft bed. I know that this is going to sound strange, but as soon as I rested my head on the pillow I felt very relaxed and my headache faded away. I think it was because the pillow coverings still had a hint of her scent, which for some reason had a soothing effect on me. I think Grandmother Katie has a presence, which lingers long after she's left. I know that sounds strange but it's true, at least in my mind it is. I closed my eyes and a short time thereafter, I drifted off into a peaceful sleep.

When I opened my eyes again it was morning. I was surprised I slept all through the night without waking up. As I became more alert I could hear the sound of raindrops splashing against the windowpane.

"It's raining pretty hard. The wind is rather high, too." The unexpected sound of Barbara's voice made me jump out of my skin. Once again she was sitting in a chair positioned in front of me waiting for me to wake up. I assumed she was waiting so that we could get into another catfight first thing in the morning. The fact that Barbara got some sort of twisted pleasure out of watching me sleep was very creepy and it made my skin feel as if there were a thousand ants crawling all over it. It was unsettling the way she could sneak up on me without my being aware of it. She was like a cat stalking a mouse. I sat up on the bed and looked at her. I didn't say anything because I didn't know what to say. I wasn't sure if I should thank her for standing up for me or prepare myself for a vicious exchange of words. Lord knows I didn't feel like fighting, but if she was looking for a confrontation, I was ready to do battle with her.

"This isn't easy for me." Barbara finally shattered the silence. "I like to have order in my life. I don't like a lot of drama and I have a difficult time dealing with change. I don't tolerate ignorance or attempts to destroy the life I've worked so hard to build and protect." Her calm tone of voice caught me off guard. I wasn't expecting her to be civil. I coiled my knees up to my chest and listened. "I destroyed your bedroom because I was certain that I'd find a stash of pills or something that would indicate you had a problem. I was also determined to prove that you were on a crusade to destroy everything I've worked so hard for."

"I'm not like that," I whispered to her.

"My heart knows that but my mind and logic are overriding what my heart knows to be true. You have to give me a little more time to adjust." There was another long and awkward moment of silence before she spoke again.

"I owe you an apology, Keysha."

"You do?" I asked, surprised.

"I judged you before I got to know you. I'm sorry I did that to you. You see, I've lived in a home with a drug user before. I know all about how abusers play tricks and how deceitful they can be."

"I'm not a drug user or a drug seller," I said, wanting to reassure her.

"I know you're not. Because if you were, by now I would have stumbled across your supply somewhere in this house or been able to detect your addiction problem." Barbara stood up and drew back the curtain and watched the raindrops fall before she spoke again. "During my freshman year of high school I looked up to my older sister, who was a junior. She was one of the most popular girls on campus. She was the party-girl type and I was pretty much a tomboy who loved sports. We had a pretty decent life. Our parents loved us, we lived in a good suburban neighborhood and we did well in school. All of our normality changed the summer before my sister was to become a senior. During that summer, she met this college guy who was attending the university that was near our home. My sister loved to brag about dating a college boy." Barbara cleared her throat. I could tell that what she was telling me was something deep and very emotional. "Anyway, my sister started hanging out at frat parties with this guy and sneaking out of the house at night to be with him. It wasn't long before he introduced her to drugs."

"Why did she take them?" I asked. "If you guys had

cool parents, a nice home and weren't struggling to make ends meet, why would she want to do drugs?"

"Peer pressure I suppose. I think she really wanted to fit in with the college crowd. She started off with pills and when that wouldn't get her high enough she began using harder drugs. It got to the point where she began stealing money from my parents in order to supply her habit. When my parents discovered the awful truth, it changed everything. They placed my sister in rehab and became overprotective of me."

"Did your sister ever get clean?" I asked, wanting to know what happened.

"Eventually, but not before damaging our relation-ship to the point that I refused to speak to her for one full year."

"What did she do?" I asked.

"The night before my junior prom, my sister had somehow gotten out of the rehab center and came home. She arrived at our door and began begging for money. When my father refused to give her money she became irate but eventually calmed down and pleaded with my parents to let her sleep in her own bed. She begged them to let her stay and not send her back to the rehab facility. She won their trust along with mine and she was allowed to stay. The following morning when I woke, I discovered that she'd stolen my mother's car along with other things she thought she could sell, including my prom dress."

"She stole your prom dress?" I asked, completely shocked.

"Yes." Barbara exhaled loudly.

I didn't know what to say after hearing that. I could only imagine how she must have felt.

"Anyway, there were other times that my sister conned her way back into the house. I eventually picked up on her tricks and where she hid her drugs."

"So when did she stop?" I asked.

"Around the age of twenty when she almost died from an overdose," said Barbara. "That was her wake-up call. She eventually got the help she wanted and needed but she took the family down a difficult road that I never want to go down again."

I took in everything that she'd just shared and concluded that perhaps she and I aren't so different in the sense that we've both been deeply wounded by people we love.

"Can I ask you a question?"

Barbara looked at me. "Yeah," she answered.

"If you had discovered that I had a problem, would you have kicked me out of the house?" I swallowed hard as I awaited her answer. She didn't take her eyes off me, not even for one second. As I read her expression I knew what her answer was before she gave it.

"No. I would have worked with Jordan to find help for you." I exhaled. It was such a relief to know that she wasn't as evil as she first appeared to be.

"I'm sorry, too," I said. "I only lashed out at you because you always seemed to be out to get me. I also want to say thank you for standing up for me in front of all those parents who were at the school board meeting. No one has ever stood up for me like that." Barbara smiled.

"Well, I think it's about time that you start benefiting from the strength of a family that cares and sticks together. We're also going to prevail in court and get to the bottom of who is trying to destroy our happy family." I swallowed hard because my heart was doing something weird. It was filling my body up with an emotion that was foreign to me.

"Um," I paused because my voice was shaking. "So you're saying that you consider me to be a part of the family?"

"Yes, I do," Barbara answered. I put my face in my hands and started crying tears of joy. Barbara came over and draped her arm around me and held on to me until I pulled myself back together.

"I'm sorry. I don't mean to be so emotional."

"It's okay to cry. Listen, I've brought up some cleaning supplies and trash bags so that we can clean up your room."

"You mean you're going to help me?" I asked, wanting to be sure I heard her correctly.

"Yes," she said with a smile.

It took a good portion of the morning for Barbara

and I to get my bedroom back in order. We had to use the mattress from Grandmother Katie's room temporarily until my mattress could be replaced, but I didn't mind one bit. When we were finished I fell in love with my room all over again.

chapter 27

Later that afternoon I went to the garage and upstairs to the workout room. Jordan was just finishing his run on the treadmill. I sat down on one of the weight machines and watched him as he wiped sweat from his face with a towel.

"Can I ask you a question?"

"Yeah," Jordan said as he stepped down from the treadmill and took a seat at another weight-lifting machine, which was next to me.

"When the results came back and they told you that I was your daughter, why did you come for me? Why didn't you just let a judge sign me over to the group home permanently and leave me there?"

"Sweetie, when I learned that you were my baby there was no question in my mind as to what my next step would be. I couldn't turn my back on you. You are my responsibility." Jordan paused for a moment and then placed his hand over mine.

"I feel cheated, Keysha. I've been cheated out of watching you enter the world, cheated out of your first steps and your first birthday. My heart is hurting about this in ways that are unimaginable. Trust me, had I known about you, believe me when I say that life for you would have been very different." I swallowed hard because my next question was a real tough one to ask. I glanced down at the floor.

"Do you—" My words got trapped in my throat. "I mean—what I'm trying to ask is, even though all this crazy stuff is going on, do you think you'll ever be able to love me?" Jordan got up from his seat and kneeled down before me.

"Look at me. Look into my eyes," he said. "I don't want you to ever think for one minute that I don't love you or that I will stop loving you."

"But I've screwed up so badly. I didn't mean to but somehow everything just went crazy," I said. I was trying to tell him how sorry I was for causing so much drama.

"You are my daughter and nothing on this earth will ever change that or the way I feel about you. Do you understand?"

"But what if we don't get a chance to really get to know each other?" I asked nervously. My worst fear was that I'd be convicted and end up in prison. "I mean, this entire drug thing doesn't make me feel good at all."

"This family is going to get through this and no matter what happens, I'm going to be there for you." I don't know why his words went directly to my heart but they did. I leaned forward, rested my head on his shoulders and hugged him.

"I love you, Daddy," I said.

"I love you, too," he answered, and hearing him say those words to me made me feel more loved and cared for than I ever had before.

READING GUIDE
QUESTIONS

1) What does Keysha want the most?
2) What are Keysha's flaws and how do you think she got them?
3) What are Keysha's strengths?
4) Is Keysha a leader or a follower?
5) What is Toya's motivation for trying to pressure Keysha to consider dropping out of school?
6) Why does Keysha still care about her mother, Justine, even after she's left her in a desperate situation?
7) While in the group home, Keysha hears stories from teen kids who were homeless and living on the streets. Discuss what you think it would be like to live on the street without food, shelter or someone to love you.
8) Discuss why you think Mike wanted to be viewed as a hard-core gangster as opposed to a clean-cut young man.

9) Discuss how and why Liz was able to connect with Keysha and get her to trust her.
10) Why do you think Jordan is willing to risk everything for a daughter he didn't know he had?

TEXT ME LIST

Favorite female artist: Alicia Keys

Favorite female group: Pussycat Dolls

Favorite female rapper: Missy Elliott

Favorite young female actress: Julia Stiles

Favorite Teen Movie: Take the Lead

Favorite Song on my iPod by a female artist:
Hips Don't Lie by Shakira

Favorite female track and field athlete:
Florence Griffith Joyner

Favorite male artist: Usher

Favorite male rapper: Yung Joc

Favorite young male actor: Mark Wahlberg

Favorite guy movie: Four Brothers

Favorite male athlete:
Muhammad Ali (the greatest of all time)

Favorite Song on my iPod by a male artist:
Justin Timberlake (SexyBack)

Favorite online site I'm hooked on for the moment:
www.myspace.com/earlsewell

Most interesting and informative Web site:
www.americaslibrary.gov

Favorite cartoon: The Simpsons

Favorite food: Banana Pudding

Favorite football team: Da Chicago Bears

Favorite basketball team: Da Bulls

Favorite baseball team: Da White Sox

Favorite season: The Fall

Favorite city to visit: Miami, FL

Favorite romantic DVD: The Piano